A  of Promises

B Y

Ana Monroy

Copyright © 2025 by Ana Monroy.

All rights reserved. No part of this book may be used or reproduced in any form whatsoever without written permission except in the case of brief quotations in critical articles or reviews.

This book is a work of fiction. Names, characters, businesses, organizations, places, events and incidents either are the product of the author's imagination or are used fictitiously. Any resemblance to actual persons, living or dead, events, or locales is entirely coincidental.

Printed in the United Kingdom.

For more information, or to book an event, contact :
ana.monroy@rocketmail.com &
https://www.amazon.co.uk/review/create-review?&asin=B0F4XYW7X7

Book design by Kindlepreneur

Cover design by Night Café

ana.monroy@rocketmail.com &

https://www.amazon.co.uk/review/create-review?&asin=B0FC6BYB3V

Book design by Kindlepreneur

Cover design by Night Café

ISBN - Paperback: 979-8286972760

April 2025

CONTENTS

1. An Unexpected Encounter
2. Terms and Conditions
3. A Whirlwind of Emotions
4. Crossed Wires
5. Ethan's Birthday Bash
6. The Morning Plans
7. Decisive Decisions
8. A Convergence of Worlds
9. Career Versus Contentment
10. Personal Realizations
11. Forging Forward
12. An Evening of Celebration
13. My Happy Ever After
14. A New Beginning
15. Epilogue Part One: A Home of Our Own
16. Epilogue Part Two: Three Years Later
    Acknowledgments
    Authors Note

1

An Unexpected Encounter

I adjusted my grip on my young nephew, Oliver, as we navigated the familiar yet slightly faded streets of my hometown. It had been years since I last returned here, and this weekend had pulled me away from my busy city life and previous work commitments. The warm spring sun cast dappled shadows on the pavement, and the scent of blooming flowers filled the air, triggering memories of my joyful childhood—a time of happiness and excitement.

As I stood beside Oliver in the café, a tall figure walked through the door, and I froze with apprehension, unable to quite make out who this man

ANA MONROY

was. While we both stood at the counter admiring the cakes and muffins on display, I gasped, finally recognizing the face—Brody, a childhood friend of the family. "Brody," I called out, "Is that really you?" "Do you remember me? I'm Ruby White, your friend from childhood. Our parents were good pals back in those days." "Yeah," Brody replied, a look of recognition dawning on his face. "Now I remember you.

You were the little girl with the blonde pigtails during the summer when my parents moved here." "So, what brings you here?" he asked, his voice filled with surprise. "I'm looking after Oliver for the weekend," I explained. "And I have plans to move closer to Oliver's family so we can spend more time together."

Brody's expression softened as he saw me with a surprised look evident in his warm smile. "Goodness, fancy running into you after all these years," he said with a flirtatious voice, brushing his hair back. I chuckled nervously, glancing at Oliver eyeing the muffins. "It's funny, I haven't been here in ages." Brody leaned against the counter with amusement. "So, you're moving back? That's a big step." I nodded; my thoughts tangled. "I have lived at home on the East Coast for so many years, so I have been thinking about moving back here to this hometown, my old former childhood hometown here in the countryside instead and reconnect with Oliver's family. Oliver is only a little once; I don't want to miss the good fun bits in his life." "Family is important," Brody said, smiling.

He seemed more grounded and mature than I remembered. "Growing up means figuring out what's really important." "Yes," he agreed. "Things don't always turn out as planned, but sometimes they turn out as they should." A pause lingered before I spoke again. "What about you, Brody? Still living here?" "Yes, I've got my own construction company now. It's a lot of work but fulfilling." "I'm glad you've found your place," I said, impressed. Brody's smile widened. "And it's nice seeing familiar faces, especially yours." We shared a quiet moment, realizing how much time had passed and how easy it was to reconnect.

Oliver tugged at my sleeve. "Can I have a muffin?" I smiled down at him, feeling Brody's comforting presence beside me. "Sure, kiddo." Brody suggested catching up over coffee. "I'd like that," I replied, smiling. As we exchanged numbers and chatted, I wondered if this meeting marked the beginning of a new chapter, where I could reconnect with my past and perhaps explore something new with Brody, including finding work.

My mind buzzed with excitement as I waved goodbye to Oliver beneath the fading light of dusk the next evening and made my journey back to the city. Upon arriving home, I sat on the front steps of my city apartment, a place that now whispered promises of new beginnings in the country town where I reconnected with Brody. That evening, the quiet murmur of the night mingled with my racing thoughts. I remembered Brody's gentle reassurance, his kind words echoing in my mind: "Sometimes, the most challenging choices lead to the most beautiful beginnings."

The following morning, I awoke with newfound hope, looking forward to my next encounter with Brody. The pull of my hometown and the memories it evoked offered a promising prospect of finding work. Over breakfast, while listening to birds chirping under the spring sun, my phone lit up with a message from Brody: "Coffee at the old corner café this weekend? I'd love to hear more about what's on your mind."

"Sure," I replied, "I look forward to meeting you this weekend at the same café without Oliver. Let's say midday?" Brody responded quickly, "Yep, that is fine with me." I felt happy to finally reconnect with my long-lost childhood friend. When the weekend finally arrived, I found myself inside the familiar, cozy café—its walls lined with vintage photographs and the soft hum of local chatter in the background—as I waited for Brody to arrive. This time, our conversation was enriched with the comfort of reminiscence and the thrill of undiscovered futures. Brody talked about the town's transformation over the years, about new faces and old traditions being revived. I shared my inner tug-of-war—my ambitious drive to move back from the city and the possibility of reconnecting with my roots in this quiet hometown countryside—Brody listened intently.

"So, what are you really looking for, Ruby?" he asked gently, his eyes searching mine with genuine curiosity. I paused, stirring my coffee slowly as if weighing each word. "I think…I'm looking for balance. A way to honour my family ties while still chasing the dreams I've always wanted. And, just maybe, get a promotion and settle down here, bringing me closer to Oliver." Brody's smile was soft and understanding, making me feel truly seen. "I believe our paths can merge—your journey, my office and home, and maybe even our shared memories. Life isn't about choosing one over the other; it is about embracing all the parts that make us who we are." In the following hours, I began to explore the old haunts of my youth with a fresh perspective.

I visited the park where I once played, reconnected with long-forgotten neighbours, and even attended a community gathering where laughter and shared history filled the air. With every step, I felt the weight of uncertainty slowly shedding away. That same crisp evening, as the town's lights flickered on and painted the streets in a warm glow, Brody and I walked through the town with an air of anticipation. Nostalgia mingled with excitement we strolled along familiar paths. Brody reached out, taking my hand in his. "I'm here, Ruby. For every step of this journey—but only if you are willing to walk it together. "Standing there, under the gentle luminescence of streetlamps and the soft hum of evening life, I felt the beginnings of something profound take root. In that moment, I realized that my future wasn't defined solely by a bustling city skyline or by the echoes of childhood memories. It was a tapestry woven from both—filled with challenges, changes, and above all, the promise of a new shared tomorrow.

As we meandered through the streets, Brody shared more about his construction company and his dreams of growing it further. I confided in him about my hopes of establishing a local accounting practice and how integrating into the community could be both rewarding and fulfilling. It became clear that our professional paths could intertwine, complementing each other's ambitions. The night ended with a quiet understanding that this was just the beginning. With Brody by my side, I felt ready to embrace every twist and turn of this unexpected, beautiful journey. Stepping into this new chapter carried the promise of a long friendship and the potential for something even deeper—an adventure I was now eager and open to exploring. The evening ended quicker than expected and Brody walked me back to where I was staying, the streets now quiet under the starry sky.

The comforting sounds of nighttime, the rustling leaves and distant chirping of crickets—wrapped around us like a familiar blanket. There was a comfortable silence between us, filled with the warmth of shared memories and the anticipation of what lay ahead. When we reached the doorstep, Brody turned to me, his expression softening under the gentle glow of the porch light. "I'm really glad we ran into each other again," he said, his voice sincere and full of warmth. "It's funny how life brings people back together just when they need it." I nodded, feeling a surge of gratitude for this unforeseen turn of events and how perfectly our paths had crossed. "Me too," I replied, searching his eyes for understanding. "It's nice to feel this connection to my past while stepping into a new future. I've been feeling so lost for a while now, and yet... it feels like I'm finding my way again."

Brody smiled, the corners of his eyes crinkling. "Sometimes, all it takes is a nudge from the universe." He paused, his gaze drifting down the street, perhaps reflecting on the twists and turns of his own journey. Then he turned back to me, with a thoughtful look on his face. "You know,

I've always admired your ambition, Ruby. You have this spark that seems to light up no matter where you are." I felt my cheeks warm at his compliment, but it also brought a sense of vulnerability. "It hasn't always felt like that," I admitted hesitantly. "Moving back here is a big step, and I worry whether I can create the life I want while finding that balance with my family. What if it does not work out?" He stepped a little closer, the sincerity of his presence grounding me. "You won't know until you try. And I believe in you. Maybe we can help each other find our way— bring our dreams to life right here in this town."

His words resonated with optimism, igniting a flicker of hope within me. I knew he was right. I had spent so long in the city chasing dreams that often felt unattainable, lost among the towering skyscrapers and endless responsibilities. Here, among the familiar sights and simpler rhythms of life, I felt the contours of my aspirations shifting, becoming clearer. We made tentative plans to meet up again soon, eager to continue this journey of rediscovery and perhaps build something new together. Brody mentioned a local community event happening next weekend, suggesting we attend together. I felt a thrill of excitement at the thought of meeting some of the locals and integrating into the community.

As Brody leaned in to give me a warm hug, I felt a mixture of comfort and something far deeper, a connection that hinted at the potential of a budding relationship. His embrace was reassuring, grounding me in the moment. "Goodnight, Ruby," he said softly as we parted, his breath warm against my cheek. "Till next time."

"Goodnight, Brody," I replied, watching him walk away, a smile blooming on my lips that I could not quite contain. As he retreated into the night, a bittersweet pang of longing mixed with excitement. It was as if he had rekindled a spark in me, one that had dimmed during my years in the city. Stepping inside, I found myself reflecting on the evening and the conversations we had shared. The walls of my current life felt less confined, more like a transition point rather than a destination. This town, once a distant memory of my youth, now resembled a canvas ready for new experiences and opportunities. I moved to the window and gazed out at the moonlit streets, imagining all the possibilities that lay before me. The threads of my past were beginning to weave seamlessly with the present, creating a tapestry rich with promise. I felt a sense of belonging and excitement about what was to come. Settling down on the couch, I pulled out my phone to jot down my thoughts.

I wanted to remember this moment—the hope, the dreams, the feeling of being alive. My fingers danced across the screen as I wrote about my newfound sense of purpose and the exciting connections I'd made. Each word spilled forth, and I reflected on how much had changed in just a short time. In my heart, I carried the weight of both my fears and my aspirations to start a career rooted in this town while nurturing my connection with Oliver and my family. With Brody's words echoing in my mind and a feeling of contentment warming my heart, I drifted into sleep, ready for whatever the new dawn might bring. As I slept, I dreamed of what could be: bustling mornings filled with laughter, afternoons spent reminiscing with Brody, and nights enlivened by the charm of the community around me. Each dream wove a future that felt both thrilling and secure.

2

Terms and Conditions

Brody leaned against his desk, observing the busy workers outside his office. The excitement was palpable, but his thoughts were elsewhere. The possibility of hiring me as a temporary accountant and future nanny seemed like inviting chaos into his orderly life, yet it also promised a much-needed balance. I was radiant that morning, with a carefree attitude that stood in stark contrast to his carefully structured life. He genuinely admired my buoyant spirit—my laughter had a remarkable ability to brighten even the darkest of days. Yet, a small part of Brody worried him that such vibrancy could disrupt the world he had built for himself. Would my presence transform his life and bring order to his business? Brody seemed ready to ask me of a possible job offer he envisaged with the company that would be perfect for me so one weekend he invited me to his office, and he asked; "Would you like to stay here with me and the business as our new accountant? Would you like me to draft a new contract?" I hesitated, snapping him from my thoughts.

ANA MONROY

With my hands on my hips, I radiated some determination and a delightful sense of seriousness, inspiring myself to embrace the unexpected. "Contract? This sounds rather serious," I remarked uneasily. "Are we to include signatures on every page next?" "Perhaps," he responded, his tone unwavering. "It is imperative that we establish ground rules to prevent any violations of boundaries." "Ground rules?" Ruby inquired nervously. "Firstly, we must maintain a professional relationship. There shall be no personal interactions outside of work, and if any issues arise, they must be addressed immediately." "Agreed," I replied, feeling both relieved and cautious as we both defined the terms of our new professional chapter.

He felt a mix of relief and disappointment in my words. Brody was glad his past wouldn't complicate things, but he also wished for a deeper connection. "Okay, I can agree to that," he said reluctantly. "What else?" I leaned against his desk. "Second, clear communication is important. No silent treatments or passive-aggressive notes. If something goes wrong, let's address it directly. We should cooperate with each other." "Fine, fine. I'll do my best. But do expect color-coded whiteboard markers." I laughed and replied, "Perfect! A touch of art to brighten up those business spreadsheets." The thoughts made Brody smile. "What have I gotten myself into?" he muttered. I spent the morning earlier meticulously transforming a corner of his office breakfast area into a cozy workspace. The gentle clink of utensils and soft murmur of conversation filled the office kitchen room as I arranged colourful notepads, markers, and a neatly organized schedule for the day. The air smelled faintly of coffee and freshly baked goods—a perfect backdrop for creativity and collaboration. As Brody emerged from the study, he exchanged a brief nod—a silent understanding of the agreement we had reached. Their arrangement was clear, fair payment terms with a clean exit plan should things ever go wrong. With that in mind, we were ready to balance both professional responsibilities and the light-hearted moments of everyday life. Brody's son, Ethan crept into the office kitchen with a bright smile, his eyes alight with anticipation. "Good morning, Ruby!"

He greeted me cheerfully, eager to join in the morning office ritual. I knelt to his level and warmly replied, "Good morning, Ethan! Today, we're going to make pancakes after work together. Are you ready to become a pancake artist?" His nod of enthusiastic agreement was the spark that set the day in motion. Later that afternoon back at Brody's house, Ethan and I got to work. I guided him through each step—measuring flour, whisking eggs, and folding in just the right amount of milk.

Brody watched from the counter, offering a supportive smile while occasionally stepping in to adjust the heat on the griddle. We worked brilliantly together, Ethan and I forgot the day's hectic work, we were totally engrossed in making tasty pancakes. I added playful touches—a sprinkle of cinnamon here, a handful of chocolate chips there—ensuring the pancakes were not just tasty but a little work of art. Despite careful planning, a small mishap occurred. The family cat, drawn by the commotion and curious about the delicious aromas, leaped onto the counter. In one swift, unexpected moment, the cat nudged a freshly prepared stack of pancakes. They tumbled to the floor in a cascade of syrup and flour. Instead of frustration, I burst into laughter. "Well, that's one way to redecorate the kitchen!" I exclaimed with a twinkle in my eye. Brody, equally amused, joined in with my light-hearted remark: "I suppose even the cat wants to be part of our creative process." Ethan giggled uncontrollably as Brody calmly gathered the fallen pancakes, ensuring not a single moment of joy was lost. The relaxed afternoon, however, was abruptly interrupted by the doorbell ringing at the front door. Brody's expression shifted slightly as he opened it to reveal a representative from the management office from the construction firm— a stern woman carrying an air of urgency. "Good morning, Mr Brody" the representative chatted away to him, her tone made it clear that this was no casual visit. She detailed concerns raised by his senior members, citing specific issues that needed immediate attention.

Inside, the warm atmosphere shifted subtly as Brody's attention turned toward resolving the emerging conflict. "I understand these concerns need addressing," he said in a composed tone, his mind already sorting through the necessary steps. I continued with the pancake making with Ehan, I was determined to impress Brody. I methodically reassembled the pancakes on a plate, also clearing up the scattered utensils and documents, ensuring that even amid external pressures, the workspace remained a symbol of our collaborative spirit.

While Brody engaged in a measured conversation with the representative—promising follow-up meetings and clear action plans— I focused on maintaining the balance of order and creativity at home. My steady presence was a reminder that, together, we could navigate even the most unexpected challenges. In that moment, the blend of making pancakes and family life revealed an exciting feeling despite life's chaos. My partnership endured interruptions and setbacks. Our adaptability and support, whether cooking at home or handling work issues, promised a future of respect, flexibility, and finding joy amid the challenges.

After the representative left, a heavy quietness fell over the house, a pause between the external demands of the day and the warmth of their shared space. Brody lingered around the doorway for a moment, rubbing his temples as he processed the concerns raised by Mrs Harrison. Across the room, I continued my work with steady resolve, carefully rearranging the pancake station and tidying up the workspace. The lingering scent of coffee and the faint aroma of syrup and flour mingled with an undercurrent of determination. Once the visitor departed, Brody stepped back into the kitchen, his expression softening as he found me gently guiding Ethan through a new pancake decoration technique. With a reassuring smile, he said, "Thanks for keeping things on track, Ruby. Today's been a bit more challenging than I expected." I offered a warm nod. "We are in this together, Brody. Even when the day throws unexpected hurdles our way, a little organization—and maybe a bit of creativity—can go a long way."

Ethan, who had been meticulously arranging sliced strawberries into what he called "pancake art," chimed in, "Auntie, Dad, look! I made a new design!" His innocent enthusiasm filled the room with a burst of energy, momentarily dispelling the morning's tension. Brody took a deep breath, allowing himself a moment of levity. "You know, sometimes I think these pancakes are like life—they might spill over, get a little messy, but they still taste great in the end." He glanced over at me, his eyes crinkled in a smile, reflecting both mischief and determination.

After breakfast, Brody retreated to his office to plan a meeting with his office colleagues, intent on addressing the issues raised and finding constructive solutions. Meanwhile, I gathered my notes and recipes, brainstorming ideas on how to use our shared passion for creative cooking to foster a stronger sense of community—not just within the household, but perhaps even with the office workers. When Brody returned later that afternoon, the air felt lighter. He found me with Ethan perched on a stool at the counter, flipping through a small notebook filled with sketches of pancake designs and ideas for an office pancake workshop outside hours. "I've been thinking," I said thoughtfully, "What if we hosted a weekend pancake session at the community centre just for the office workers and their families? A little event where everyone could join in the recipes, and even learn a thing or two about finding joy in the unexpected?" Brody's eyes lit up at the suggestion. "That is a brilliant idea. It could be a way to bring us all together and ease some of the tensions around here—and maybe even build a bit of a reputation for us but also for my fellow co-workers." Ethan clapped his hands in delight. "I want to help! I can show everyone my dinosaur designs!" he exclaimed, the innocence of his excitement was a reminder of the simple joys they had been striving to preserve. As dusk settled over the town, Brody and I sat together on the porch, watching the sunset paint the sky in hues of gold and pink. The events of the morning had been a stark reminder of life's unpredictability, yet here we were—finding solace in each other's presence and in the small, meaningful moment that punctuated their day.

In that quiet twilight, Brody reflected aloud, "It seems no matter what chaos comes our way, there's always a chance to reset—to turn a spilled pancake into something beautiful." I reached for his hand; my voice was soft yet resolute. "We may not have all the answers right now, but together, we can face whatever comes our way. Even if that means a few more spilled pancakes along the way." And so, with plans for a community pancake workshop taking root there was a renewed sense of partnership, the day's challenges began to fade into the promise of a future built on collaboration, creativity, and the willingness to embrace both one another despite the occasional delightful mess from that morning with Ethan.

3

A Whirlwind of Emotions

I entered the bright, buzzing community centre earlier that day, excitement coursing through me as I prepared to lead a parenting workshop alongside my colleagues from the office. The anticipation of sharing my insights with parents and children filled me with purpose. As the workshop began, I felt assured in my dual roles, seamlessly blending my professional prowess with my nurturing instincts. I spotted Ethan, with his usual exuberance, running ahead in his beloved dino socks. Seeing him so animated warmed my heart, his vibrant energy mirrored the creativity I had been experiencing at work, all thanks to the confidence Brody's support had given me. "Ruby! Ready for another engaging day?" called one of the other parents, her voice filled with camaraderie as we moved toward the activity room dotted with interactive stations.

"Absolutely! I am looking forward to experimenting with new ideas both here and back in the office," I replied, my tone brimming with excitement. As I guided activities with a natural ease, I recognized how my experiences leading office meetings effortlessly translated into facilitating group activities with families. It felt exhilarating to bridge the gap between my worlds. Meanwhile, I noticed Brody standing nearby, and I could not help but admire him as he observed me leading the workshop. Watching me command the room and inspire not only the children but the parents too filled him with quiet admiration. I realized how our contrasting approaches—his structured nature complimenting my warmth and creativity—strengthened our connection both in the community and through our collaborative work endeavours. "Remember to keep it light and fun!" I suggested during a storytelling exercise, imitating animal sounds to spark laughter. Brody, despite his usual hesitance, soon found himself swept up in that moment.

"Give it a go, Brody!" I encouraged him, my eyes twinkling with mischief. His smile grew, and as he embraced the silliness, I felt a rewarding satisfaction watching him engage with Ethan in these new ways. It felt like a deepening bond growing between us, reflecting not only our personal relationship but also our shared aspirations at work. While assisting with crafting activities, I took a moment to reflect on how far we had come. My thoughts drifted back to how I had watched Brody's confidence bloom in both personal and professional spheres.

Yet, amid the joy of the day, a passing comment from another parent brought back a swirl of complex emotions. "Ruby, you are a natural. He is lucky to have someone nurturing like you," the parent remarked, nodding appreciatively towards Brody and Ethan. The remark stirred something within me.

While I cherished my role in Ethan's life and the journey I was sharing with Brody, the implications of being viewed as a maternal figure sent ripples through my heart. What boundaries were being crossed, and what did this mean for my feelings for Brody? I glanced at him, now engaged in another lively conversation with Ethan. His easy laughter and relaxed demeanour spoke volumes about our shared journey, and I recognized the beauty in what we were building together.

As the workshop wound down and families began to leave, the connection I felt with Brody remained strong. He leaned closer to me and asked, "Want to grab a coffee at my place?" His voice carried a casual comfort that made me smile. "Sure, that sounds great," I replied, grateful for his steady presence, my heart tugging at the intricate dance of affection that had begun to flourish between us. When we arrived at Brody's home, he loosened his tie and pulled me close to him. I could feel the warmth of his body and the rapid beat of his heart, and in that embrace, I surrendered to the moment.

With each gentle kiss, a ripple of energy coursed through me, igniting a sense of belonging I had never anticipated. This connection with Brody felt utterly transformative, filled with a profound sense of love. We kissed, I felt a wave of desire wash over me, longing to explore every part of this man. Brody took my hand and led me to the bedroom, where we sank onto his king-sized bed. His fingers traced the contours of my half-dressed body, each touch igniting a blossoming warmth that spread throughout me.

I responded with equal fervour, our chemistry manifesting in an intimate dance that was both exhilarating and comforting. "Brody," I breathed, my voice barely above a whisper as I leaned in closer, our lips brushing against one another. "You make it so easy to lose yourself at this moment." "That's the magic between us," he replied, brushing his thumb gently along my jawline, his gaze unwavering as it locked onto mine. "You bring out the best in me." The passion enveloping us was palpable, saturating the air with an electric energy as we ventured deeper into each other's warmth. With Philip Glass' piano melodies softly playing in the background, it was to fit together, each kiss and touch deepening the emotional connection we had forged. As we lay entwined in the soft sheets, I felt the tension of the outside world melt away, leaving just the two of us cocooned in love and the promise of our shared journey.

Brody's hands, warm and reassuring, explored freely along my back, igniting a spark of excitement with every gentle graze. "I want to build a life with you, Ruby," he murmured, his voice husky with emotion. "I want us to be partners in everything—our careers, our dreams, and our family." His words made my heart flutter. I pulled away slightly, searching his eyes for sincerity. I found it there—deep admiration mingled with something more profound. "You and Ethan mean everything to me, Brody," I replied, feeling my voice thick with emotion. "I never imagined I could find this kind of connection. But I want to make sure we navigate this together. I do not want us to lose sight of our individual passions or feelings for one another."

As Brody nodded with his expression steadfast, he said in a soft voice, "We will not lose each other. I promise. Our dreams will elevate each other, and I will always support you, no matter where your journey takes you." Emboldened by our shared commitments, I leaned in once more, capturing his lips with mine—a kiss filled with promises of what was yet to come. The world outside faded into the background as we delved deeper into our connection, our bodies moving in perfect harmony under the soft light.

Each caress and whispered word became a testament to our evolving bond, reinforcing how profoundly we complemented one another. Shortly as the night unfolded, we lay together in the flickering candlelight, the stars shining through the window. I nestled into Brody's side, wrapping my arms around him, feeling safe and cherished. The night transformed into a celebration of our love, each moment solidifying the foundation of a life that would thrive on romance and chemistry. "I can't wait to see what the future holds for us, Ruby," Brody said softly, running his fingers through my hair, his eyes twinkling with affection. "Neither can I," I replied, my voice thick with emotion. "Whatever comes next, I know we'll face it together."

Just then, the soft sound of the wind rustling through the trees outside whispered promises of possibility. In that intimate cocoon, I realized that we had truly come full circle, anchoring ourselves in love and ambition as we prepared to dive into the adventures that awaited us.

As I lay there beside Brody, the soft rhythm of his heartbeat served as a soothing lullaby, lulling me deeper into contentment. The amber light flickering from the candle illuminated the room, casting gentle shadows that danced across the walls as if mirroring the warmth that filled my heart. My thoughts danced between the joy of our connection and the promise of a future that felt both thrilling and secure, one that I had not fully dared to envision until now. I reflected on how far we had come—transforming from colleagues to friends, and now to something much deeper. Our relationship had blossomed from shared laughter in the office to heartfelt discussions about life, love, and our aspirations for the future. Each moment we spent together seemed to knit our lives closer, intertwining our dreams and hopes into a beautiful tapestry. The sense of partnership we were building felt both exhilarating and grounding.

Outside, the world lay cloaked in night, a tranquil silence reigning with the stars twinkling down at us like gentle reminders of the endless possibilities that lay ahead. I marvelled at the idea that we had embarked on this journey together, not just in our personal lives but professionally as well. With plans of community workshops, joint projects, and shared family moments on the horizon, I realized how intimately intertwined our lives had become.

The soft sound of the wind rustling through the trees outside created a soundtrack of serenity that washed over me. I could not help but smile as I envisioned the adventures that awaited us—weekend getaways filled with laughter, late-night brainstorming sessions over cups of coffee, and quiet evenings spent in each other's arms. There would be challenges and hurdles to overcome, no doubt, but with Brody by my side, I felt a newfound confidence in tackling anything that came our way. The warmth of his presence made me feel a surge of gratitude for all the experiences that had led me to this moment.

The uncertainty and solitude I had experienced before felt like distant memories. In their place stood hope and directional clarity of purpose I had long sought. Brody was not only my partner in business; he was also the anchor that grounded me emotionally, the person who believed in me and inspired me to become my best self. The continued flickering of the candlelight etched a soft glow around us; I turned slightly to face him.

Our eyes met, and in that moment, I saw a reflection of my own feelings mirrored in his gaze. It was a silent communication that transcended words—a promise that we were embarking on this journey together, no matter where it might lead us. "Tomorrow holds endless opportunities," I whispered to him, feeling a surge of affection as I traced my fingers gently along his arm. "I can't wait to see what awaits us."

His lips curved into a smile, and he pulled me closer, his warmth enveloping me in a cocoon of safety. "Whatever it is, we'll face it together," he replied, his voice low and reassuring. "I have no doubt we're capable of creating something incredible side by side." Feeling the weight of his words and the sincerity behind them deepened my appreciation for our bond. I planted a soft kiss on Brody's forehead, the intimacy of the gesture encapsulating all the warmth I felt in my heart. "You mean a lot to me, Brody. Thank you for being you," I murmured, hoping to convey just how significant he had become in my life. While my eyelids grew heavy from the peaceful atmosphere, I gradually surrendered to the embrace of sleep. Dreams began to swirl in my mind, painting vivid pictures of the future I hoped to cultivate—with Brody and Ethan by my side. I envisioned laughter echoing through the house, the aroma of fresh pancakes filling the kitchen, and moments of quiet togetherness shared over cups of tea. The night wrapped around us like a cozy blanket, and I realized that this was just the beginning of something truly extraordinary—a life where we could build dreams together, anchored in a love that would only grow stronger with each passing day. With a final contented sigh, I let myself drift further into slumber, filled with anticipation for the promise of tomorrow and all that it would bring.

ANA MONROY

4

ANA MONROY

Crossed Wires

Brody sat at the head of the conference table, rubbing his temples as he attempted to focus on the agenda in front of him. The aftermath of the office workshop felt like a whirlwind, and all he could think about was my contagious laughter, my vibrant ideas, and the warmth that had seamlessly enveloped his little family. Yet, alongside those joyful thoughts brewed an unease, a fear of the shift I was bringing into his life. The more he tried to reel in those feelings, the more they tumbled out of control. He felt unmoored, standing on the precipice of change, resisting the pull as if he might fall into an unknown abyss. As he turned his attention back to the board meeting, the office colleagues discussed the latest financial projections, but all he could envision was my enthusiastic pitch about organizing a community pancake workshop with him and Ethan imagining his son playing dinosaur battles in his living room. "How do you want to proceed with this budget allocation, Brody?" asked Lisa, his office secretary, snapping him out of his thoughts. "Uh, right," he said, fumbling for the figures I had just moments ago studied with Brody. I glanced at the account number sitting at a table nearby but all I could see was his bright smile and the joy he brought into my life. "I think we should adjust some funds toward… um… innovation initiatives—"

"Innovation?" Lisa raised an eyebrow. "Brody, are you pulling that from somewhere, or was this influenced by our earlier conversations?" Her question lingered in the air, heavy with implications that made the other team members exchange glances, their discomfort palpable. Heat rushed to my cheeks from what I overheard. "It is important to engage with our community and explore new avenues.

If we do not take steps toward transformation, we risk stagnation," he replied, trying to sound confident while he was fully aware he was veering off course. "Sounds a lot like something your new accountant Ruby might be able to help you with," someone remarked, their tone echoing through the conference room. "Yes, right!" he mumbled, annoyed at the relentless connection they were trying to draw. "It's just—" "Brody, does she have you wrapped around your finger or something?" Lisa teased, a smirk curling at the edges of her lips. "Of course not! It is not like that," he insisted, the dismissal rolling off his tongue more defensively than he intended. He caught me glancing at him down the table, where he suppressed a knowing smile. But deep down, he felt the tug of truth in his playful jibe. Ruby was softening him in ways he did not think possible, making him reconsider how he should approach both life and work. Was that a good thing, or was it opening him up to vulnerabilities that could lead to trouble? After the meeting wrapped up, he returned to his office, the weight of distraction trailing closely behind me. While settling down in just that same instance his assistant, Maggie, popped her head around the office door frame, a playful glimmer in her eye. "What's going on with you today?" she asked, crossing her arms. "I can practically see the little hearts flying around you. Did Ruby sprinkle magic dust onto you?"

"Very funny, Maggie. I am just focused on my work," he replied, attempting to maintain a façade of professionalism while internally grappling with the truth of her observation. But Maggie's teasing continued, and her expression softened. "Look, I am just saying, you have been a little less preoccupied with work these days, and well, it is nice! Who does not love Brody with a bit of levity?" "Just focus on your own work," he said, irritation creeping into his voice, but he could not hide the smile forming on his lips. As Maggie turned to leave, her laughter echoed behind her, and his thoughts began swirling again.

Could it be that Ruby had an impact on his attitude and approach to life? He had not let anyone in since his marriage had fallen apart—a thought that sent a quick shiver down his spine. Memories flooded back—moments of strain, feelings of betrayal, and the lasting impact of a broken family. Did Ruby's growing presence threaten his resolve to protect Ethan from that same pain?

His thoughts spiraled before another noise pulled him from my melancholy—his phone buzzing with a familiar tone. His heart sank when he saw the name flashing on the screen. "Jessica…" he whispered, uncertainty flooding in. He had not heard from his ex-wife in months. What could she possibly want? With a mix of hesitation and resignation, he answered, "Hello?" "Brody," Jessica's voice came through, cool and composed, but it carried an edge of urgency that set me on high alert. "I hope I'm not interrupting anything important, but we really need to talk." "Is everything okay?" he inquired, with a hint of worry rising within him. "What's going on?" "It is about Ethan. We need to discuss his upcoming birthday party," she replied over the phone. The somewhat casual tone in her voice brought forth a flood of memories—of planning, stress, and reminders of his past marital strife. He exhaled slowly, feeling a wave of apprehension wash over him. "We talked about this already.

ANA MONROY

I thought we agreed on a joint celebration with my family and yours. It is the easiest way to manage it." "Joint celebration is still in play, but I have a couple of ideas that might be better received with the new arrangements. I did not want to catch you off guard, but I have been speaking with someone about the party planning, and things have changed," Jessica said with a clear tone in her voice. "What changes? You are not throwing this into another spiralling chaos, are you?" he felt his frustration bubbling just below the surface. He had hoped his communication would be easier after their last contentious discussion. "I had some discussions and thought we might want to consider a bigger venue—the usual spot wouldn't do anymore, especially with how many of Ethan's friends are expected," she offered, hastily rationalizing her decisions. "Jessica, the budget was already tight, and I did not want to shift it at the last minute. What are you suggesting?" His voice strained with tension. "I am suggesting we collaborate with someone new— someone who has connections to turn this party into something memorable! Support in finding promotional partnerships could help!" Her excitement spilled over the line.

The mention of partnerships twisted in Brody's gut, mirroring exactly what was happening with the office workshop ideas with mine. "Partnerships can interfere with visions, Jessica. What is more important? A big show of a party or ensuring that Ethan is happy with something simple?" "Brody, at least consider it. I also know more about Ruby' idea of her community workshop… It would be good for my image too to get involved" Jessica stated smoothly, thinking that the revelation would pacify him. He stiffened at her last remark, feeling a sharp annoyance clawing at him. "Are you really tying Ethan's birthday party to corporate image? This is not about us—it is about him!" "Exactly! It is about him, but it is about making sure we stay connected no matter what," she insisted, but I could sense the undercurrent of tension in her tone.

We continued to debate, but with each exchange, he felt more entrenched in growing frustration, fuelling my internal conflict about me and the feelings he still struggled to understand. Brody thought back to the warmth and excitement he felt during the workshop and how Ruby had sparked a light in his hectic life. Why was it so difficult for Jessica to see that? "Look," he finally said, his voice firm, "I want to put Ethan first. Let us get through this. We will meet to talk about the party details later, but I will not compromise on what he deserves." "Fine," Jessica snapped, the tension palpable through the phone. "But you'd better think this through, Brody. You have a habit of putting up walls." With that, the call ended abruptly, leaving him staring at the phone in frustration. The echoes of the conversation replayed in his mind, wrestling with his emotions as he leaned back in his chair.

Just then, I walked back into the office, having finished speaking with the workers for the workshop gathering. "Is everything alright?" he asked, noticing my furrowed brow. He forced a smile, the weight of the call still hanging heavily around him. "Just some family complexities. You know how it goes." "Does it have to do with Ethan's birthday?" I asked, his voice taking on a more serious tone. "Yes," he admitted, his voice hesitant. "But it's complicated." I stepped closer, my tone softening. "You can talk to me, Brody. I am here for that. I want to support you through this." As I stood there, warmth radiating from her presence, I felt the same walls he had constructed around his heart begin to solidify. The unspoken feelings and budding affection he harboured for me clashed with his responsibilities as a father. "Thanks, Ruby," he said, trying to keep his expression neutral even as emotions roiled within. "I appreciate it. I really do." But as we stood there, that moment of warmth quickly slipped away, replaced once more by the weight of his responsibilities. It felt like the barriers he had erected to keep his personal life separate from his professional obligations were resurrecting themselves, closing off the connection that was just beginning to blossom. "Brody, are you sure you're all, right? You seem... distant,"

I pressed with concern as I searched his face for answers. "I just had a conversation with Jessica, my ex-partner," he confessed, feeling a current of frustration surge back. "She is all over the place with Ethan's birthday plans, trying to make it some grand event. It is like she does not understand what really matters."

I nodded with a neutral expression. "That must be tough. It is hard when co-parenting becomes a tug-of-war. But you are his dad, and you know what he needs." "Exactly," he replied, breathing deeply. "But when Jessica starts making it about her image rather than what is best for Ethan... it throws me off. And now, with the pressure from work and everything else, I feel like I am losing control." "Brody," I said softly, stepping closer, "You are doing the best you can. Just try to focus on what you want for Ethan, not what anyone else expects—not even Jessica." Her words sunk in deeper than I anticipated, igniting a flicker of confidence in me. I recalled the laughter and warmth we had shared during the workshop and how much I wanted that same joy for Ethan.

"Thanks," he murmured again, gratitude infusing his voice. "It helps to know someone has my back." As Ruby smiled, a weight began to lift, and he allowed himself to breathe a little easier. Just as I thought we were finding our way, Ethan bounded into the room, excitement radiating from his small frame. "Dad! Aunt Ruby! Can we build a fort now?" he begged, bouncing on his feet. "Of course!" Ruby replied, instantly transforming into the playful figure Ethan adored. "We will need some blankets and pillows! And do not forget the dinosaur plushies!" As I closed the office for the afternoon, we all made our way home to unwind. He watched my effortless connection with Ethan, a tender warmth blooming inside of me. Seeing her create a safe and joyful space for his son made him realize how lucky he was to have her in his life. As they built the fort together, laughter and giggles filled the room, mingled with chaotic enthusiasm. I playfully threw pillows at Ethan, and as I held the blankets to form the fort walls, I felt a genuine sense of happiness.

"Watch out! Here comes the T-Rex!" Ethan shouted, running around us in a playful frenzy. "Quick, defend the fort!" I yelled in return, clearly revelling in the joyful chaos. But as I joined in, the sound of our laughter gradually faded into the background and my nagging doubts crept back into my mind. I wanted this warmth and connection with Brody but how long could we dance around the reality of his responsibilities? Just then, the familiar chime of my phone interrupted the fun, and he glanced at the screen, his heart sinking when he saw Jessica's name flashing across it again.

He muttered under his breath, "Ugh, not now," hesitating to pick up the call. I noticed the shift in his demeanour and asked gently whether it was Jessica again. He nodded, feeling torn between the light-hearted atmosphere we had created and the weight of reality pressing down on us. "I should probably take this," he told me. "I'll just be a minute." he encouraged himself to go ahead, his voice soft yet firm. "I'll keep Ethan entertained," I assured him, and he stepped into the hallway to take the call, unable to shake the sense that this moment was pivotal for his relationship with Ruby and his struggle to balance his role as a father and a professional.

"Hello," I answered, trying to keep my voice steady as he distanced himself from the laughter and warmth in the room. Jessica's voice came through, unmistakably serious, and the gravity of her tone set off alarm bells in my mind. There was an urgency in her words that made it clear things were not right on her end. As she launched into a discussion about the need to finalize the birthday party plans for Ethan, he felt a surge of irritation rise within him. He wished he could push aside the tension swirling around our lives, but it seemed impossible, Jessica emphasized her expectations and the complications in her plans, frustration bubbled over. I was aware of the promises I'd made and the commitments I was supposed to uphold, but the pressure felt unbearable. He could feel the walls closing in, pushing away the light he had brought into his life, just as Jessica's words began to twist and pull at his resolve. With every exchange, Brody felt more entrenched in frustration, tangled up in the contradictions of wanting what's best for Ethan while navigating the complexities of co-parenting with Jessica. The idea that Jessica could perceive Ruby as overshadowing our relationship frustrated him immensely. He wanted to protect the light Ruby brought, on both him and Ethan, that sentiment resonated deeply inside Brody as he stood in the hallway, the laughter of the fort-building session echoing faintly behind him. Jessica's sharp reminders about expectations weighed heavily, and the conversation began to twist further into chaos. In the end, my patience frayed.

He could see that his life was becoming a delicate balancing act, teetering between the past and present, with Ruby's illuminating paths he never thought he would dare to explore. The complexity of it all loomed over him as he faced the reality of his situation. And as he ended the call abruptly, he found himself standing there, wrestling with emotions that left him feeling more vulnerable and unsettled than he had expected.

ANA MONROY

5

Ethan's Birthday Bash

The sun shone brightly on the day of Ethan's birthday, casting a warm glow over Brody's backyard, which had been transformed into a festive wonderland. Colourful streamers danced in the gentle breeze, and a giant inflatable dinosaur loomed proudly at one end of the lawn. I stood at the centre of the organized chaos, tying balloons together with nimble fingers, my heart racing with anticipation and excitement. "Are the cupcakes ready?" Brody called out, glancing toward the kitchen window where I was busy preparing the last treats. "Almost! They just need a little more time!" I responded, infusing my voice with enthusiasm that mingled seamlessly with the celebratory spirit of the day. I could hear the distant chatter of guests arriving, their laughter blending with the joyous sounds around me. Ethan was running around, overflowing with energy, darting between family and friends as they arrived. "Auntie!" he shouted at one point, pausing mid-sprint to look back at me. "Is everyone going to love the party?" "They are going to love it, sweetie! Just wait until they see your dino fort!" I reassured him, my fondness for Brody's son evident in every word.

Watching how effortlessly I connected with Ethan filled me with warmth, and I felt at home in this moment. It was moments like these that made me wish this could be our everyday reality, yet a pang of uncertainty flickered at the back of my mind—what would my future at work look like? As the last guests trickled in, I spotted Jessica moving about, chatting with some family members. The tension from her earlier visits loomed still, and I hoped today would bring moments of joy rather than conflict. I felt a mix of anxiety and anticipation rippling through me.

Jessica seemed relatively passive today, but I could sense the underlying tension in the air, making me hyper-aware of how easily the dynamics could shift. "Hey, Ruby!" Jessica greeted me suddenly; a bright smile plastered on her face. "Everything looks lovely. I appreciate you handling so much of this." "Thanks, Jessica!" I responded, keeping my tone upbeat, even though I sensed my sincerity felt strained. "We just want today to be special for Ethan." "Of course," she replied, but I caught a flicker of something in her gaze, a hint of possessiveness that threatened to pierce my confidence. As the party officially began, I led a round of games filled with laughter and joy, my spirit soaring as the children engaged in dino-themed activities. Ethan's laughter rang out, pure and bright, filling my chest with affection. When it was finally time for cake, I could feel the excitement in the air reach a new peak. It was the moment they had all been waiting for, and I helped Ethan blow out the candles on his cake—a glorious creation decorated with colourful dinosaurs and sparkling candles. "There's one for each of your friends!" I exclaimed, leaning in closer to Ethan, feeling his excitement radiate beside me. "Make a wish, buddy!" "Good job, Ethan!" Brody encouraged with pride, watching his son close his eyes tightly, brow furrowing with concentration.

Once the cake was cut and everyone gathered for dessert, I felt a rush of happiness seeing the smiles on the children's faces. Engaging with the parents, sharing laughter and stories, pulled me deeper into the community I was beginning to embrace. Just as I settled into the warmth of the moment, Jessica interjected, her presence looming like a dark shadow. "Don't you think we should save some of the cake for when he opens his gifts? You know how parties can get chaotic." I noticed Brody glance at me, a flicker of irritation passing across his features, but he kept his tone steady. "We will manage, Jessica. Let us focus on enjoying the moment right now."

Ethan's face lit up at the idea of gifts, and I quickly redirected the conversation. "You are right! Let us gather around for Ethan to open his presents! We can save some cake for later!" As the group moved to gather around, I could feel the tension tighten in Jessica's expression. My heart raced as I sensed how easily this celebration could spiral into conflict. "Ethan, are you ready?" I called out, excitement bubbling in my voice. "Yeah! Gifts!" Ethan shouted, his face lighting up with glee as he tore into the first present, revealing a shiny new toy. The room erupted into cheers as he held up a T-Rex triumphantly, eyes sparkling with joy.

ANA MONROY

"Look, Dad! It is a T-Rex!" he exclaimed. "That is awesome, buddy! The best birthday gift ever!" Brody said, grinning proudly. I felt a surge of happiness as I took in the scene—the connection between father and son felt palpable and genuine, fuelling my own affection for them both. Ethan moved quickly to the next gift; a beautifully wrapped box adorned with colourful paper. "Open it! Open it!" the other children shouted, their excitement fuelling his eagerness. "Yes! Let's see what is inside!" I encouraged, clapping my hands together to heighten the anticipation. As Ethan expertly tore open the wrapping, I could not shake the feeling that the atmosphere around us was near perfect, filled with laughter and love. But just as I began to settle into the warmth of the moment, Jessica's voice cut through the joy. "Ethan, make sure you save some room for the cake. We would not want you to spoil your dinner." "Mom! I can eat cake anytime!" Ethan protested, rolling his eyes playfully but clearly excited about his new toy.

"Yes, but I want you to be able to enjoy it later. We must keep things on schedule!" Jessica insisted, her firm demeanour casting a sudden chill over what had been a lively gathering. I exchanged a glance with Brody, who appeared equally troubled by Jessica's interruption. He tried to maintain a sense of calm, his eyes searching the room for support. "Let's just enjoy the opening of gifts for now," he said, his voice carrying a gentle authority that managed to sway the mood back toward laughter. "Ethan deserves that, don't you think?" Ethan nodded vigorously; a grin plastered across his face as he continued to dive into present after present. With each unwrapped gift came cheers and applause from the children, their energy infectious.

I watched the chaos unfold, feeling an exhilarating sense of belonging as I revelled in their joy. Then came the moment Ethan opened his art set. A spark ignited in his eyes, and my heart swelled as I imagined all the creative projects he could tackle with it. "That is great! Can we make a dino mural?" Ethan asked with uncontainable excitement. "Absolutely! We will have to work on that together," I replied, trying to keep my voice upbeat, even as a knot tightened in my stomach. As the party continued, I noticed Jessica talking quietly to some of the other parents, casting sidelong glances toward Brody and me. The tension felt palpable, and I could not shake the sensation that Jessica was quietly orchestrating a plan to undermine the happiness we were all trying to cultivate. Finally, as the time for cake approached, I felt the weight of the impending moment settle in. The cake adorned with colourful frosting and dinosaur figurines sat waiting, yet an underlying sense of dread crept in as I noticed Jessica's expression—a mix of determination and calculation. Attempting to redirect the atmosphere, I suggested, "Let's make a toast."

ANA MONROY

I wanted to bring attention back to the celebration. "To Ethan—to family, friendship, and making memories together."

Everyone raised their glasses, and their voices filled the air in a chorus of goodwill. However, I could still sense the tension lurking beneath the surface. Brody looked at me, and I noticed a flicker of unease shadowing his features, as if unresolved issues were threatening to unravel the joyous occasion. The candles on the cake flickered brightly, Ethan leaned forward, eyes gleaming with anticipation. "Can we all sing before I blow out the candles?" "Absolutely! On three!" I said, leading the room in song, my heart soaring with the energy of celebration.

However, just as we finished singing and the atmosphere felt buoyant again, I could not ignore the intrusive thought creeping back into my mind—Brody's decision to offer me a new job stirred feelings of excitement, but Jessica's controlling nature threatened to pull my happiness away. Once the candles were extinguished, laughter and cheer returned to the room briefly, allowing me to revel in the moment. I turned to Brody to share in the joy, but my heart sank as I caught sight of Jessica staring at us, her expression unreadable. The tension thickened, and I felt a knot tighten in my stomach again.

"Brody!" Jessica called out, her voice rising above the cheerful chaos. "Can I speak with you for a moment?" Brody hesitated, glancing back at me, concern etched across his features. "Yeah, just a second," he replied reluctantly, setting aside the cake platter as he stood up. My excitement drained slightly as I watched him follow Jessica to the side of the yard, their heads bent low as they engaged in a hushed conversation. The joy that had filled the air moments ago felt like it was slipping away, replaced by uncertainty and tension. "Is Dad going to be, okay?" Ethan asked, his excitement dimming as he looked up at me, sensing the shift in the atmosphere. "I hope so, sweetie. Sometimes adults just need to talk about things," I reassured him, though I could feel my own anxiety beginning to gnaw at my heart. I started to wonder if it would always be like this— the interruption of happiness by unresolved conflicts from the past. Watching Brody Walk away with Jessica felt like a shadow creeping over the party, dimming the vibrant energy that had previously filled the backyard. I knelt to Ethan's level, forcing a smile onto my face to alleviate his concern. "Hey, look at all these amazing gifts you're getting!"

I pointed to the pile of colourful wrapping paper and boxes scattered around. "Let's see what else is waiting for you!" Ethan's eyes brightened, his excitement rekindling as he clutched his new dinosaur toy. "Can we play with all of them later, Aunt Ruby?" he asked, his innocence shining through. "Absolutely! We can have the best dino adventure ever!" I replied, my heart warmed at his enthusiasm. I tapped into that same energy, hoping to divert any lingering tension. As Ethan excitedly dug into another present, I forced myself to look away from Brody and Jessica. I wanted to dismiss the thoughts swirling over the impending discussion and their implications, but the nagging concern lingered.

I continued to engage with the other parents, sharing laughter over stories of their childhood experiences and how much fun it was to participate in events like this for their kids. However, each time I glanced over at Brody and Jessica, I noticed the way Jessica leaned in closer to him, her body language exuding possessiveness. I could feel the corner of my heart tightening with frustration and uncertainty. I did not want her to overshadow the happy atmosphere we were trying to create for Ethan's special day and watching them interact began to feel suffocating. Just then, some of the other parents began to gather around, bringing more laughter back into the air.

Someone made a joke about their own birthday experiences, and that got everyone chiming in with tales of chaotic birthday parties. I breathed a small sigh of relief as their enthusiasm began to drown out the noise of tension. But the moment did not last long. Just as I was feeling a sense of belonging wash over me again, I noticed Jessica shooting glances our way, eyes narrowed as if she were surveying a territory she intended to reclaim. The smile I had been wearing felt fragile now, as if it could crack at any moment. I tried to focus on Ethan—his innocent joy was my primary anchor—but I could not help feeling torn.

This party was supposed to celebrate him, but the undertones of Jessica's presence loomed ever larger. "C'mon, buddy! Let us see what else you have got!" I encouraged Ethan, breaking into his world of excitement again. He quickly tore through another present, revealing a set of dinosaur-themed pyjamas. "Look! Now I can be a dino when I sleep!" His laughter rang out, and I felt a swell of pride at his ability to find joy even amidst the chaos.

We continued the gift-opening frenzy, I glanced back at Brody and Jessica, whose conversation was getting intense. I could see Brody's furrowed brow; he looked like he was trying to keep the peace. My frustration ignited again, threatening to extinguish the joy emanating from the kids and our cozy gathering. I wished desperately that Jessica could leave well enough alone for the sake of Ethan's happiness. Eventually, I found the courage to approach Brody while carrying a wrapped gift that Ethan had just opened. "Hey, could you come over here for a second?" I called, trying to keep my voice light, even though uncertainty curled in the corners of my mind. He turned away from Jessica and walked over to me, a mix of relief and hesitation evident on his face. "Everything okay?" he asked, his brow still slightly knit as if the tensions had yet to dissipate. "Ethan is doing well with his presents. He needs his dad's help to tackle this gift," I said, holding the box up toward him with a smile.

Brody's smile broadened as he glanced at Ethan, who was waiting eagerly for him. "Of course! What is in that one?" he asked, looking back at Ethan, his demeanour shifting into the playful father I admired. Just before Ethan could rip into the box, Jessica called out from a distance. "Brody, we need to finalize the birthday arrangements!" There it was again, that sharp edge in her voice that cut through the happiness. I felt my heart sink momentarily. Brody hesitated, glancing back at Jessica, and then at me. I could see the conflict dance across his face—his paternal instinct tugging him towards Ethan, while obligation pulled him back toward Jessica. "Just a second, Jessica," he said firmly, turning his focus back to Ethan. "Let's see what's inside, buddy."

Ethan grinned widely, practically bouncing on his feet as he tore away the wrapping. Inside was a set of building blocks embossed with dinosaur prints, and his squeal delight filled the air, contagious enough to spread to everyone around. "This is the best!" he shouted, his tiny hands fumbling with the box as he eagerly pulled the blocks out. Brody knelt beside him, excitement reflecting in his eyes as he helped Ethan line up the blocks, preparing for the next round of imaginative play. "Look, Dad! We can build a dino fort!" Ethan exclaimed, his imagination already running wild. I could not help but smile at the sight, feeling a warmth swell in my chest. Watching them together was a reminder of the bond they shared, a connection that filled me with hope for what our little family could become. The room erupted with laughter and joyful chatter as other children rushed over to join Ethan, eager to contribute to the construction of this dino fort. I stepped back, taking a moment to observe the scene—the colourful chaos, the booming laughter, and the festive decorations swaying gently in the breeze.

It was a picture of pure happiness, one that seemed to dance in perfect harmony with the carefree atmosphere surrounding us. Just then, Brody caught my eye from across the room, a broad smile stretching across his face as he shared in the joy of the moment with Ethan. In that instant, I realized how deeply I had come to care for both, how intertwined our lives had become within this celebration. Despite the undercurrents of tension that still lingered from my earlier interactions with Jessica, I allowed myself to breathe, to savour this slice of joy. As the kids continued building the fort with shouts of delight, I felt renewed determination brewing inside me. I dreaded the conflicts that loomed on the horizon, but if I kept my focus on the warmth of this shared experience, perhaps that light could guide us through darker moments. Today was a celebration of Ethan, yes, but it was also a celebration of the bonds we were forming, the laughter shared, and the hope that tomorrow could be just as bright.

ANA MONROY

The Morning Plans

Brody stood in the kitchen, feeling a surge of confidence as he surveyed the space around, which was transforming into a familial haven. The gentle scent of freshly baked cookies filled the air, a delightful reminder of the joy shared with Ruby White, some days before. Today was the day he'd finally declare his commitment to me, in making me a permanent part of his world. This moment felt pivotal—a chance to convey just how much I meant to him. He seamlessly integrated himself into my life, his spontaneous energy reinvigorating both Ethan and me. As I thought about his bright spirit and unwavering optimism, I felt my heart quicken. I was not just a new addition to the company but someone who had become an auntie figure to Ethan but also a loyal friend. More than that, I held the potential to transform this romantic relationship with Brody into something more permanent. Just then, he entered his home office, a playful smile gracing his lips. "Are you ready for our big planning session at the office in town?" he asked, holding up a colourful notebook and a set of markers while sipping coffee, his enthusiasm spilling over. "Ready as I'll ever be," I replied, trying to muster an upbeat tone. Yet even though the morning was filled with anticipation, I sensed the weight of uncertainty pressing down on me, particularly regarding my role as his accountant and what our future might hold. "Great! I have been thinking about how we can expand our community workshop ideas to reflect our values," he continued, trying to channel his excitement into my plans.

My eyes began to sparkle with enthusiasm as I flipped open a notebook while listening to what he had to say. "I would love to hear your thoughts. You always know how to make these ideas feel real," he said. I was feeling the walls he had built around us start to crumble. Brody had a remarkable gift for bringing down barriers, making me more susceptible to the warmth he radiated. It was both exhilarating and terrifying letting him in had awakened my feelings I had long buried, and while that felt alive, it also filled me with uncertainty.

"I think we're ready to present our ideas to the board," he said thoughtfully, focusing on the task at hand. "Showing our expertise will create a genuine connection and prove we're thinking about the business's best interest." "That's a strong angle," I replied, and as we worked on the presentation details, the scent of his aftershave enveloped me, easing the knot of anxiety broiling inside of me. I could not help but feel that each moment we spent together was weaving an ever-growing tapestry of shared goals and intertwined feelings, an exhilarating connection that made our heart race. But just as he was caught up in this blissful momentum, his serious tone brought me back. "Ruby, I really want to talk more about our future. I know the workshop project is important, but what about us? Where do you see us going?" The question hung in the air, charged and heavy. I opened my mouth to respond, but the right words slipped away, he struggled to articulate the truth that felt so close yet so daunting. "I care about you, Ruby. You have changed how I view family and connection," he finally managed to say, his eyes searching for understanding. "Brody, I appreciate your concern, I really do. But I need to know that you can trust me, that we are on the same page, not just at work but as friends," she said earnestly, wishing for him to know how genuine her feelings were. "I want that too," he said, leaning forward, his openness encouraging me.

Despite the complexity of their histories, he felt a deep yearning to embrace what was blossoming between them. Just then she gathered her thoughts to express to him what she truly felt, then a sharp buzz of her phone jolted me out of the moment, sending a shiver down my spine. "Perfect timing, isn't it?" I muttered, annoyance creeping into my voice as I glanced at the screen. The notification was from the office; it was insistent, urgent, I felt a heaviness settle over me. "It looks like work has other plans." "Ruby, you don't have to answer it right now," Brody urged, concerned about shadowing his features. "I should see what it is; it might be important," I said, though regret began to swirl within me.

Just when I thought there was a breakthrough, the pressures of responsibility started to weigh down on me. I took a deep breath and reached for my phone, the atmosphere shifted again, charged with anticipation and anxiety. "Brody…" I whispered, her voice carrying a weight that pulled my attention back to his. I turned to look at him, seeing the concern written all over his face. The moment felt heavy with unspoken words and possibilities, making my heart race with the realization of everything we had shared so far. I swallowed hard, torn between the responsibilities awaiting me and the burgeoning feelings I had for Brody. The connection we shared felt like a beautiful promise, yet everything could be threatened if I let work overshadow this moment. Taking a shaky breath, I pushed back the frustration and opened the email, scanning its contents. It detailed an escalating situation regarding an acquisition attempt at the office, along with urgent requests from the board for immediate insights and decisions. "Ruby?" he urged with concern evident as he searched my face for answers. "Is everything okay?" "Just another work issue," he replied vaguely, feeling the words taste bitter on my tongue. He wanted to push the message aside, but the urgency gnawed at him, insisting that he address it before it spiralled out of control. The world felt like it was narrowing around him, and he could feel the sense of dread grip his heart again.

His hopeful gaze anchored me momentarily, but the atmosphere thickened with tension as he stared back at the doorway, trying to shake off remnants of unease. "Ruby, I need to address this. I cannot just ignore what's happening," he said, his voice edged with uncertainty as he turned away from me, focusing on the email in front of him. "Brody, whatever it is, can it wait," I urged gently. "I am about to share something important with you. We have worked so hard to build this connection—do not let it slip away because of work obligations." His words resonated deeply within me, and for a moment, my resolve wavered. The warmth that had enveloped us moments ago felt so inviting, yet the looming responsibilities I faced on all sides threatened to pull me back into my shell.

I wanted nothing more than to embrace the connection we were forging, to dive into the feelings that had blossomed so unexpectedly between us. He took one more look at his phone, he felt the urge to dodge the distraction and focus solely on me. "You've opened my eyes to so much more than I thought possible," he confessed, my heart pounding in my chest as he stepped closer, wanting desperately to close the distance between us. "You've breathed life back into my world." His eyes softened, and a flicker of understanding passed between us. In that moment, my heart swelled with the anticipation of finally voicing how he felt—but before he could articulate the profound emotions surging within himself, the doorbell rang again, jolting us both from the chatter we had been creating. "Seriously? Who could that be now?" he groaned, frustration resurfacing as he glanced at the doorway.

I looked at Brody with a mix of concern and encouragement. "Maybe it is just a delivery. Let it go," he said softly, though he could see himself with a worried expression in his eyes. But the pull of responsibility nagged at him he could not ignore it. "I'll get it," he said, suppressing the mounting anxiety as he walked toward the door. He hoped that we could focus on the moment of connection together, but the unexpected interruptions felt like a constant struggle against progress. When he opened the door, his heart sank at the sight of his neighbour Sam, an urgent expression plastered on his face. "Brody, we need to talk about our backyard shared fencing—" he started, but Brody felt irritated, and he realized that he did not have much time for this now. "Sam, I really do not have time for this right now. Maybe later?" he replied tensely, feeling bewildered. Before he could step back inside, I approached Brody from behind, his presence grounding me. "Brody, we should hear him out. If it is about the backyard, it could affect our plans." He paused for a moment; caught between the responsibilities of his neighbour and the warmth of the connection we had made together.

"Fine. Let us hear what he has to say," he finally relented, knowing that it was best to address things that could further interfere with our lives. Just as he was preparing to discuss it with Sam, a loud crash sounded from the backyard, sending a rush of adrenaline through Brody and myself. "What was that?" Brody exclaimed; his eyes wide with concern. "Ethan!" he shouted instinctively, adrenaline surging as he rushed past Sam. I could sense that his heart was pounding fast as he raced towards the source of the noise, my mind racing with worry for his son.

I followed close behind, my determination fuelling the urgency as we both burst into the backyard. There, we found Ethan standing frozen, knuckles pale against the edge of a toppled garden chair, which had clearly fallen and created the disruption. Brody knelt beside him, relief flooding through me as he asked, "Ethan! Are you all, right?" Ethan looked up at him with wide eyes trembling a little as he clutched a blanket. "Yeah, Dad. It just fell over!" "Thank goodness," he said, wrapping Ethan in a reassuring hug. His heart steadied as he hugged Ethan closely grounding the little boy in the moment. As I moved forward to stand beside Brody in the backyard, I took the courage to kneel beside Ethan, my expression shifting from concern to a warm smile. "You scared us there, buddy!" I said, ruffling Ethan's hair playfully. "I'm glad you are okay. How about we check the fort to make sure it is still standing?" Ethan's excitement returned as he nodded vigorously, eager to ignore the earlier fright. "Yeah! Let's go see!"

He grabbed my hand, pulling me towards the makeshift fort we had all built earlier, the energy and laughter returning to his face like a ray of sunshine breaking through clouds. As I followed, I felt a sigh of relief escape my lips. Remembering myself interacting with Ethan was a sight that filled my heart with warmth. I found a way of transforming any moment into a joyful adventure, and I realized just how integral I had become to both Brody and Ethan's lives.

Brody stood back for a moment, observing the two of us, Ethan crawled into the fort with me, our laughter ringing out, filling the backyard with happiness. In that moment, I felt the weight of the world lift slightly, the pressures dissolving in the face of such pure joy. But deep down, I still could not shake the fear of what would happen next—how the complexities of Brody's relationship with Jessica might overshadow these precious moments we were creating. It felt as though we were teetering on the edge of something beautiful and vulnerable, caught between hope and uncertainty. Courageously, he approached me, I made a silent vow to protect our newfound happiness. "Hey, guys! What are we building now?" he called, joining with excitement as he crouched beside the fort. "An even bigger dino fort!" Ethan said, his eyes were shining. "Perfect! Let's make it the biggest and best one ever—just like the dinosaurs would have wanted," he chuckled, feeling the bond between me and Ethan which began to solidify. His face expressed with a grateful look, and for a moment, he shared an unspoken understanding of the importance of a solid partnership—not just as a playful father but involving me, the new aunt figure into this family. Two adult people navigating the complexities of commitment and love together.

In the laughter, chatter, and playful chaos of that special day, the threads of my life intertwined in a way that was meant to be. For the first time in a long while, I sensed that, just maybe, the future could offer something extraordinary for me—a family built not only on the remnants of the past but on the bright possibilities of today and tomorrow.

As the sun continued to shine and Ethan's laughter echoed around us, I took a deep breath, ready to face whatever challenges might come our way. Together, we were constructing a new chapter—one filled with creativity, love, and hope. And gazing at Ethan, the warmth of that moment filled his heart, reaffirming his belief that true connection is worth fighting for. With those thoughts anchoring him, he threw himself into the infectious energy of the afternoon, eager to build not just forts and dreams but a life rich with love and shared experiences. No matter what obstacles lay ahead, I felt ready to tackle them, confidently in having me by his side and fueled by Ethan's joy lighting the path forward.

ANA MONROY

7

Decisive Decisions

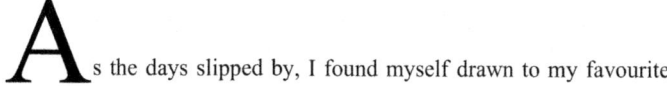s the days slipped by, I found myself drawn to my favourite café at the corner after work. The familiar scent of freshly brewed coffee enveloped me in a comforting embrace as I flipped open my journal. The bustling noise of conversations and laughter around me created a cocoon of warmth, but the swirl of uncertainty in my mind felt anything but tranquil. Today, I was torn between two worlds—my lucrative job at the office awaiting me and the newfound joy I had discovered in Brody and Ethan's home.

I took a deep breath, letting the rich aroma of coffee calm my racing thoughts, and began to write. *What do I really want? I penned, swirling the ink across the page. *Is it the job or is it the life I've built here? The question lingered as I wrestled with why leaving my previous city felt like losing a part of me. My thoughts flowed freely onto the paper, capturing the deep conflict I felt in my heart. It became clear that it was not just about the job; it was about the connections—laughter, moments spent wandering around the living room with Ethan, and those quiet glances shared with Brody that made me feel seen and valued.

Just as I finished a particularly poignant line, the café door chimed, and I looked up to see Brody step inside. The moment our eyes met, I felt a surge of warmth, even amidst the tension lingering from the chaos of the past few days. "Hey," he greeted, moving toward me with that genuine smile that momentarily stole my breath. "Mind if I join you?" "Not at all! I was just… thinking," I replied, tucking my journal out of view, hoping he would not notice the hesitation in my voice. Brody settled into the chair across from me, a casual ease in his demeanour that made my heart flutter and palms sweat. "You looked a little pensive. Everything okay?" he asked, his expression softening with concern. "More or less," I said, forcing a smile. "Just contemplating life choices, you know?" "Heavy stuff for a café," he replied, a teasing glint in his eyes. "But you can't escape those choices forever." "True.

I suppose that is what I am wrestling with," I confessed, feeling the weight of my thoughts shift as I gazed into his eyes. "It is just… I am torn between wanting this job and what it would mean for us." Brody leaned forward his expression serious. "What do you really want, Ruby? Does the job outweigh what you have found here?" His question hung in the air, pressing against my resolve. "I love being here—I truly do. But I worry that my decision to stay is tied to more than just my career prospects," I admitted, my voice barely above a whisper. "I don't want to base my choices on personal feelings, especially if I'm not certain how you feel about… us." Brody's eyes widened slightly, surprise flickering across his face. "You think it's just about the job?"

"No, I don't," I rushed to clarify. "But sometimes, I can't help but wonder if I'm stepping into something deeper or just becoming dependent on what you and Ethan bring to my life." Brody's expression softened, and I felt my heart race as I laid my feelings bare. I watched him closely, longing to see how he would respond, but the moment felt charged with possibilities—both thrilling and terrifying. "I'm glad you're here," he began, his voice steady. "You've become a significant part of my life and Ethan's… and I think about what that means." Just as my heart raced with anticipation for something more, his phone buzzed loudly on the table, shattering the charged atmosphere. Brody's expression shifted to annoyance as he glanced down at the screen, his brows knitting together.

"It's my office," he said, clearly torn between wanting to prioritize our conversation and responding to the urgent call. "I have to take this." "Of course," I replied, disappointment crashing over me like a wave, but I tried to keep my tone light. "Work comes first, right?" Brody nodded, his eyes lingering on mine for a moment longer, tension crackling in the air. "I'll be right back," he promised, turning away. As he stepped away to take the call, I felt a mix of emotions swirling inside me, the visceral longing clashed with mounting frustration.

Just when we were on the brink of addressing our feelings simmering beneath the surface, an uninvited interruption pulled him away. I bit my lip, watching as he moved to a quiet corner of the café, his expression shifting to one of focus as he answered the call. I forced myself to look around, trying to distract from the electric energy lingering between us. The scent of coffee filled my senses, and I watched as a mother laughing with her child at a nearby table, their easy affection reminding me of the warmth I had just begun to experience with Brody and Ethan. Yet, deep down, uncertainty gnawed at my insides. What if Brody would always place his professional obligations above our growing relationship? What if my feelings for him were deeper than I had acknowledged, pushing the boundaries we had set? The questions threatened to overwhelm me. After a few moments that felt like an eternity, Brody returned, a furrowed brow still etched across his forehead. "Sorry about that," he said, the weight of the call evident in his tone. "I am going to have to head back to the office for a bit. There is an issue they need me to address." "Is everything okay?" I asked, a sense of dread creeping in, I was concerned about Brody. "Just some updates about the investigation they mentioned," he replied, his voice tense. "I'll fill you in later."

My heart dropped slightly. This was a challenge we were meant to navigate together, yet the mounting tension felt insurmountable at that moment. "Okay. Just be careful out there. We will figure out whatever is going on when you get back." He nodded, holding my gaze for a brief second that felt electric, but then it faded as he slipped back into the role of the focused executive once more. As Brody prepared to leave, the warmth of our earlier conversation felt distant. I watched him go, the small group of parents and children continuing around me, their laughter contrasting sharply with the uncertainty filling my heart. Suddenly, the café door chimed again, pulling me from my thoughts. A familiar face walked in—Jessica, Brody's ex-wife.

Her demeanour was composed but exuded an air of authority that made my stomach twist. "Ruby," Jessica said with a tight smile, her eyes scanning the café as if searching for something or someone. "I didn't expect to find you here." "Hi, Jessica," I replied, my voice steadier than I felt. "What brings you to this part of town?" "Just a quick stop. I am looking for Brody; I need to speak with him about Ethan's birthday plans. It is important," she stated, her tone leaving no room for ambiguity. I felt a pang of unease at the mention of those plans; it reminded me of the complexities that loomed over our situation. "He just stepped out for a work thing. I am sure he'll be back soon," I said, trying to keep my voice neutral, but the tension was palpable. "Of course," Jessica dismissed me with a wave of her hand, her attention turning away.

The aloofness only intensified my anxiety. I knew this woman's presence could threaten the fragile balance we were trying to build. Then, the door swung open again, and Brody returned, looking slightly frazzled but determined. When he saw Jessica and me together, a shadow of concern crossed his face. "Jessica! I was not expecting you here," Brody said, his voice tightening as he approached. "I just need to go over the arrangements for Ethan's drop-off and pick-up at the nursery during the week with you. We should finalize the details," she said briskly.

Brody stepped closer, casting a sidelong glance at me, sensing the tension in the air. "Can this wait?" "I'd like to talk about our plans with Ethan right now as we discussed earlier on the phone," Jessica replied. "No, it can't wait any longer, Brody!" Jessica argued sharply, creating immediate strain. "These plans are important for both of us, and we need to work together, remember?" I felt my insides twist at the implications of Jessica's words, my earlier confidence slipping away. It felt like our sanctuary was under siege. "Jessica let's not do this here," Brody said, frustration creeping into his voice. But Jessica pressed on, her eyes glinting with a strange mix of determination and possessiveness. "I want to make sure Ethan has the best time with both of us, Brody.

It's not just about you and Ruby." The harsh tables of their past loomed around us, and I could feel my cheeks flush with irritation. "Excuse me?" I interjected, my voice steady despite the burning in my chest. "I think Brody and Ethan's happiness should be the priority; I'm only trying to help them both by giving my wholehearted support." Brody shot me with a quick look, concern flashing across his face. "This isn't the time for this," he whispered harshly. Jessica pressed on, her tone sharp. "Maybe you should think about the boundaries you are crossing. Isn't it risky to be so involved?" I felt my pulse quicken, my heartbeat loud in my ears as I met Brody's painful expression. Moments ago, we were on the verge of clarity, sharing our thoughts and acknowledging our growing connection. Now, though, the conversation had veered into uncertain territory, teetering on the edge of something volatile. Brody opened his mouth to respond, but the weight of Jessica's words hung heavy in the air. The warmth I had felt earlier was replaced by a chill wrapping itself around us. The tension crackled between us, suspense thickening as neither of us found the courage to bridge the growing chasm. "You know this isn't simple," Jessica continued, her voice unwavering. "We all have responsibilities. Maybe it is time to reconsider what you're doing."

I swallowed hard, battling the urge to defend myself. How had this turned into an interrogation? Just as I was about to speak, Brody's voice cut through the stillness. "We'll figure it out," he said, though the uncertainty in his tone was impossible to ignore. The atmosphere felt suffocating, every second stretching uncomfortably as I shifted in my seat, seeking an escape from the oppressive conditions. "It's getting late," I suggested, my voice carefully measured. "Maybe we should finish this conversation another time." I reached for my things, desperate to steady my nerves. But just then, my phone buzzed in my pocket. Pulling it out, I read the notification flashing across my screen: Official Job Offer: Immediate Response Required. The timing could not have been worse.

The reality of the decision I faced collided violently with the fragile state of my relationship with Brody and the current tension with Jessica. I felt the weight of it pressing down on me. Accepting the offer could mean leaving behind the delicate connection I had just begun to build. Rejecting it might mean turning my back on an opportunity back in the city that I had been working toward for so long. I glanced at Brody again, my heart racing as unspoken questions hung between us. Jessica remained unmoving, her presence a constant reminder of the complexities that filled our lives. The air thickened with the gravity of what lay ahead. My heart pounded as I stood at the crossroads of my choices, realizing that no matter which path I chose, nothing would remain the same.

Brody's eyes, filled with uncertainty, met mine, while Jessica seemed to radiate disapproval, her earlier words echoing in my mind. In that moment of chaos, I took a deep breath, struggling to gather my thoughts. There was so much at stake—my career, my relationship with Brody, and the life I had built around both. My fingers trembled as I hovered over the "Accept" button on my phone.

"Ruby, I…" Brody began, his voice faltering as if searching for the right words. "I don't want to see you go if this is what you really want, but I also can't ask you to sacrifice your dreams for us." Jessica interjected, her tone softening just a fraction, "Maybe it's time you did what you need to do for yourself." Yet her words carried an edge, hinting at the deeper conflicts that lay beneath the surface. I looked between them, one a pillar of support, the other a force of ambition.

The café was thick with tension, each second reminding me that time was slipping away. With a shaky exhale, I knew I had to decide. I pressed a key on my phone. "I'll need some time," I murmured, my voice barely clear over the roar of my thoughts. "I can't decide right now." Brody nodded slowly, his expression unreadable. "Take all the time you need. I will be here." Jessica's gaze remained steady, almost resigned. "Just remember that every decision has its consequences." As I stepped back from the table, it felt as if the ground beneath me was shifting. The decision was not just about a job—it was about defining who I wanted to be and what kind of life I truly wanted to lead. Would I chase the professional pinnacle that the job represented, or embrace the uncertain, heartfelt promise of staying close to my hometown roots and to Brody? I left the café, the heavy silence swirling around me, giving way to the distant hum of the town outside.

Each step echoed the uncertainty of my future. Back in my apartment, I sat alone with my thoughts, the phone message open on my desk like a silent challenge. The coming days would force me to confront not just my ambitions but the delicate tapestry of relationships I had woven over the years. In the solitude of that moment, under the glow of the moonlight streaming through my window, I understood that every promise, every decision would lead me closer to the person I was meant to become, even if it meant embracing both the joy and heartache of the journey ahead.

I lay in bed that night, my mind racing through possibilities, each path branching out like the roots of a tree. The crossroads lay before me, its path uncertain yet brimming with potential. I whispered a quiet promise to myself: that no matter which way I turned, I would remain true to my heart, weaving together the threads of my life into a tapestry that honoured every promise made along the way.

The next few days passed in a blur. I tried to immerse myself in my work, but the weight of my decision lingered like a shadow. Each time my phone buzzed, my heart raced, hoping it might be Brody reaching out; however, it was often just work-related notifications pulling me back into the reality I was trying to escape. I met with Ethan and Brody as much as I could, cherishing those moments. Watching Brody interact with Ethan reminded me of what we had built together, the small, tender moments of family I had found in them. Yet with every laugh we shared, there was a growing gnawing in my stomach, a constant reminder of the decision looming over me. One afternoon, as I sat on the park bench watching Ethan play, Brody arrived a little later than expected. "Sorry I'm late," he said, breathless and slightly dishevelled. "I had a long meeting. It was long." "It's alright," I replied, forcing a smile. We shared a quiet moment, watching Ethan energetically running around. The laughter and joy emanating from him felt like a warm balm on my worries, if only for a moment. "Have you thought more about the job offer?" Brody asked, his tone cautious but curious. I felt the knot in my stomach tighten. "I have," I admitted, "but I just... I don't know, Brody. Everything is so confusing right now." I looked at him, my heart twisting. "I don't want to make a decision that could change everything between us." Brody's expression turned serious. "I understand. But you deserve to go after what you want—whether it's this job or a future with us. You should choose what will make you happy." "But what if I can't have both?" I challenged myself gently. "What if pursuing my career means losing this connection with you and Ethan?"

"Sometimes you have to take risks to find what's truly worth it," he said, his gaze unwavering. "I care about you, Ruby. Whatever you decide, I want you to know that I will support you." His words flickered like hope in my heart, but the cold fear of losing him was equally tangible. "What if what I want means leaving you both behind?" I asked with a steady voice. "What if I end up regretting my choice?" Brody smiled softly, his expression reflecting an understanding that felt profound. "Regret comes from not taking the chance when you have it.

I want you to know that no matter what happens, I value our time together. It is something I'll always treasure. Just promise me you will not close any doors without truly considering what is on the other side." With those words hanging in the air, I faced a decision that felt larger than life itself. A few days after our conversation, I finally decided to meet with Brody about the plans for Ethan's birthday. I felt a surge of determination as I realized, in that moment, that I wanted to embrace my future while still nurturing the relationships I had grown to love. When I arrived at the café, I was surprised to see Brody sitting at a table, already looking serious as he pulled up the plans from his phone. "I'm glad you're here, Ruby," he said, relief washing over his features at my arrival. "We need to talk about some important decisions regarding Ethan's birthday." "Absolutely," I said, taking a seat across from him, my heart racing. "But I've been thinking about our conversation, too." He looked up, a mixture of anticipation and apprehension on his face. "What do you mean?" "I mean about the job offer," I started, my heart pounding in my chest. "I want to pursue it, but I also want to make sure that I am still here for you and Ethan. I am committed to being a part of your lives. I do not want my professional ambitions to take me away from you." Brody's eyes widened with surprise and then softened, a smile creeping onto his lips. "Are you saying you're going to accept the job?" "I want to explore it," I replied. "But I also want to make it work with you. I believe we can still have what we have built together while I chase my dreams."

I paused, feeling the weight of the hope in my voice. "I need your support, and I want to navigate this together." Brody leaned across the table, resting his hand on mine. "I am here for you, Ruby. We will figure out how to balance it all together. Ethan will love having you around for his birthday, and I will make sure you are included in everything. For the first time in days, I felt a lightness in my heart. The swirling uncertainty that had consumed me was slowly giving way to hope, and I realized that navigating this new reality would not have to mean sacrificing the relationships I cherished.

As we discussed the details of Ethan's birthday celebration, I could see the excitement in Brody's eyes. He spoke animatedly about his plans, and I found myself mirroring his enthusiasm, my earlier worries fading to the background. It felt good to collaborate on something meaningful, to share in the joy of creating a special day for Ethan. "Let's make it a memorable one," I suggested, my voice gaining strength. "We can organize games, have a cake with all his favourite superheroes, and make sure his friends are involved." Brody nodded, his smile widening. "That sounds amazing! I love that you're so invested in this. It means a lot to both of us." At that moment, as we focused on the silly details that come with planning a child's birthday, I felt a renewed sense of purpose. I could pursue my career while still being part of Brody and Ethan's lives—no decision had to be mutually exclusive. "Thank you for being so supportive, Brody," I said softly, meeting his gaze. "I want this to work. I really do." "Me too," he replied, sincerity saturating his voice. "Whatever it takes, we'll make it happen—together." As we wrapped up our plans, I realized that this journey was about more than just the job offer; it was about carving out a life that encompassed both my ambitions and the love I had found. No matter what the challenges that lay ahead, I felt more prepared to face them.

Later, as I walked out of the café, the sun setting in a wash of golden hues overhead, a smile crept across my lips. The road before me was still uncertain, but I was ready to embrace it, confident that with Brody and Ethan by my side, I could create the life I wanted. I was no longer just at a crossroads; I was stepping confidently onto a path that was uniquely my own. And for the first time in a long time, I had the power to choose. As I turned down the familiar street toward my apartment, I could not help but feel that whatever came next, I was ready to face it head-on, with a heart full of hope and a spirit determined to soar.

ANA MONROY

8

A Convergence of Worlds

ANA MONROY

The golden haze of late afternoon spilled through the front windows of Trattoria Fiore as I stepped inside, the air warm with the scent of garlic, tomatoes, and wood-fired bread. I'd always liked this place—something about its cracked tiles and mismatched chairs that made it feel real. Honest. Exactly what I needed right now. I spotted a small table tucked near the back, lit softly by a low-hanging lamp and set for two. The waiter smiled when I asked to be seated and handed me a menu I barely glanced at.

I already knew what I wanted. Something familiar. Something grounding. Red wine and spaghetti. I ordered the bottle before Brody arrived, needing something to take the edge off the nerves coiling in my stomach. So much had happened in the past few days—emotions unraveling in cafés, conversations left half-finished, choices still hovering unanswered in my phone's inbox. And then Jessica. That confrontation still echoed in my chest, like a bruise I kept poking. By the time I saw Brody walk through the door, I felt a strange mix of relief and anxiety. He looked tired, like the world had leaned on him too hard this week. But when he spotted me, his face softened—just a little—and my heart did that impossible thing it always did around him. "Hey," he said, sliding into the seat across from me. "Hey," I replied, pouring him a glass of wine. "You made it."
"Wouldn't have missed it."

We didn't speak for a moment, the silence between us settling like a soft blanket. The kind you only share with someone who's already seen you at your most uncertain. "Spaghetti and wine?" he asked, lifting an eyebrow. "Comfort food," I replied. "Figured we both needed it." He nodded slowly. "Good call." When the plates arrived, we ate in quiet appreciation, the kind that made it feel like the meal mattered less than the company. I twirled my fork absently; my appetite was slow to arrive.

"I've been thinking," I said eventually, the wine loosening the words that had been stuck in my chest all day. "About everything. The job. The offer. Us." Brody set his fork down. "Yeah. Me too." "I feel like I'm being pulled in two directions. The job is everything I thought I wanted. But this life I've found here—with you and Ethan—it's more than I ever expected. And now I'm scared that whatever I choose... I'll lose something important." He leaned forward slightly, his gaze steady on mine. "You don't have to choose between one dream and another, Ruby. Maybe you just need to figure out how to carry both." I looked down at my plate, the steam rising in soft spirals. "But what if I can't? What if trying to do both just means I end up failing at both?" "Then we try again," he said. "Together." His words caught me off guard. Simple. Quiet. Full of weight. I looked up, studying his face—every line of concern, every unspoken promise etched into the curve of his mouth. "I don't want to walk away from you," I said. "But I also don't want to give up on the woman I was before I came here. The one who fought to get her foot in the door. The one who wanted more." "Then don't," Brody said, his voice low but sure. "Don't give her up. Bring her with you. She's part of this too."

A silence fell between us, but this time it wasn't heavy. It was thoughtful. Shared. I reached for my glass and took a slow sip, feeling the warmth settle into my chest. "Do you really think we can make it work? If I take the job, I might be travelling. I won't always be here." "I think," he said, "if something matters enough to both people, they find a way." I let his words sink in, settling like roots in the uncertain soil of my future. I didn't have all the answers yet. Maybe I wouldn't for a while. But sitting there with Brody, sharing pasta and red wine in the fading light, I realized that love didn't always come with roadmaps or timelines. Sometimes it just asked you to show up. Fully. Honestly. Brave enough to admit when you were scared. "I want to try," I said, voice barely above a whisper. "Whatever this is, Brody... I want to see where it goes."

His eyes softened, and he reached across the table, taking my hand in his. "Me too." And just like that, the noise in my head quieted. The decision wasn't solved, not yet. But for the first time in days, I felt like I didn't have to face it alone. The two worlds I had been torn between weren't colliding—they were starting to converge. Maybe this was how something new began—not with certainty, but with a shared willingness to find out what could be possible. As we left the restaurant, the sky bled into soft amber hues, the town alive with the buzz of early evening. We walked side by side, our fingers brushing once, then slowly lacing together. I didn't know where the path ahead would lead—but for the first time, I was okay with that. Because sometimes, you don't need all the answers. Just the courage to keep walking together. Brody's hand in mine felt like an anchor—warm, grounded, steady. I looked down at our intertwined fingers, noticing the way his thumb moved absentmindedly against my skin. There was no music playing, just the hush of soft conversation around the restaurant, punctuated by the occasional clink of cutlery. We were surrounded by people, but it felt like we existed in our own pocket of time. "I used to imagine what success would feel like," I said quietly, almost to myself. "I thought it would be loud. Shiny. Like walking into a room and everyone knowing you belonged there." "And now?" Brody asked, his voice careful, coaxing me gently out of my own head. "Now," I exhaled slowly, "I think it's quieter. More like… coming home to yourself. Knowing what you've built has meaning—even if no one else sees it."

He didn't speak right away. Instead, he let the moment breathe, gave it space to unfold. "I think you've always known what matters," he said eventually. "You just forgot to give yourself permission to want both." I stared into my glass, the wine catching the dim light like a pool of garnet. "Is that selfish?" I asked. "Wanting both?" Brody's answer was firm, immediate. "No. It's brave." I swallowed hard, the lump in my throat catching me off guard. My appetite had mostly vanished, the spaghetti cooling on the plate in front of me. But the wine warmed me from the inside out, and Brody's presence—his patience, his willingness to just sit in this with me—made it easier to breathe. "I don't want to lose myself," I admitted. "Not to a job. Not to a relationship. Not to fear." "You won't," he said. "Not if you stay honest with yourself. And not if we stay honest with each other." There it was again—that *we*. That word that used to scare me and now felt like hope wearing real clothes. He made it sound so simple. But I knew it wasn't. We had his job. Jessica. Co-parenting. His whole world already built before I ever walked into it.

"You know she doesn't want me around," I said, not needing to say Jessica's name out loud. "I saw it in her eyes. Every time she speaks to me; it's like I'm intruding." Brody leaned back in his chair, rubbing a hand across his jaw. "She's… complicated. And guarded. And yes, she's territorial when it comes to Ethan." "I get it," I said. "She's, his mum. She's been in your life for years. And I'm just—" "Don't," Brody interrupted gently. "Don't do that thing where you shrink yourself to make others more comfortable. You're not 'just' anything. You matter to me. You matter to Ethan. And if Jessica has a problem with that, we'll deal with it." I blinked quickly, pushing back the sting of tears. His voice was low but steady, filled with that quiet conviction I'd come to depend on. It wasn't a grand declaration of love, not yet—but it was something real. Something strong enough to stand on.

"I just don't want to be the reason things get harder for you," I whispered. Brody shook his head. "Things have always been hard. You didn't cause that. If anything, Ruby… you've reminded me of what it feels like to want more than just getting through the day. You make me want to be better. For myself. For Ethan. For you." The words settled in me like a stone sinking into still water. Not explosive. Not dramatic. But deep. And lasting. For a while, we both just sat with it—him tracing circles on the tablecloth with the base of his glass, me watching the last of the sunlight slip down behind the rooftops beyond the window. The world outside moved on. We sat still. "Would you hate it," I asked, breaking the silence, "if I took the job but stayed rooted here? I mean... if I tried to do both?" "I'd hate it if you gave up a part of yourself for anyone," he said. "Even me. But if you stay because it's what *you* want, and not because you're afraid... then no. I wouldn't hate it. I'd be proud of you." A breath I didn't realize I'd been holding slipped out of me. The tightness in my chest loosened. "Okay," I said softly, feeling the word ripple through me like a pebble skipping across water. "Okay." Brody reached across and tucked a strand of hair behind my ear. "We don't have to solve everything tonight." "I know," I said. "But I needed this. I needed you." He gave me a look I knew I'd remember. One of those rare ones—tender and full of that quiet sort of love he never said aloud but sometimes showed without meaning to. "We'll figure it out," he said. And for the first time in days, I believed it. Later, as we finished the last sips of wine and the waiter brought over the bill, I felt something shift. The rest of the world would still be complicated tomorrow.

The job offer would still need an answer. Jessica would still hover, and the future would still be hazy. But for tonight—for this moment—it was just us. Red wine. Empty plates. Soft light casting golden shadows across the table. A convergence of two very different lives. And maybe, just maybe, a beginning. As we stepped out into the street, the dusky sky had shifted to a deep indigo, and a hush had fallen over the town. The hum of passing cars and the faint scent of jasmine in the breeze felt oddly poetic—like the world was pausing with us, holding its breath. Brody walked beside me, close but not pressed, our hands brushing occasionally, as if we were still figuring out how to hold each other again after all that had been unsaid. I glanced over at him, silhouetted in the fading light, and felt something quiet and powerful stir inside me—a sense that maybe the pieces of my life didn't need to compete anymore. Maybe they could *layer*. My ambition and my heart, my independence and my desire to belong, the future I dreamed of and the present I was learning to trust. For the first time, I realized it wasn't about choosing a world. It was about having the courage to build one that belonged to me—and inviting someone into it who wouldn't ask me to choose. Not between them, not between anything. Just a life made whole by presence, by intention... and by love, no matter how quietly it arrives.

ANA MONROY

9

Career Versus Contentment

I stood before the window at the office, my eyes tracing the vibrant colours of the sunset as they bled into the horizon. The big-city job offer sat on the table behind me; its glossy presentation was a stark reminder of the ambitions I had harboured for years as an accountant. It beckoned me with promises of prestige, opportunity, and the chance to elevate my career to new heights. Yet, as I weighed it against the intimacy of my life I had built with Brody and Ethan, a tumult of emotions surged within me, battling for attention. The stability I had found within the warmth of their home felt precious, a tapestry woven with shared dreams, laughter, and a sense of belonging that filled my heart to the brim. However, the nagging temptation of a successful career began to stir doubts—the fear that pursuing love meant sacrificing my professional aspirations. Could I truly make peace with setting aside what had always been a significant part of my identity? I turned away from the window, glancing back at the table. The thought of completely letting go of this opportunity filled me with dread. What if this life with Brody was a fleeting moment of happiness? What if I put my faith in our relationship only to watch it dissolve in the face of ambition? Amidst my internal turmoil, my heart ached for clarity. "Brody," I said softly as I approached him, watching him work at the dining table. "Can I talk to you about something important?" He looked up, his eyes warm with concern. "Of course, Ruby. What is on your mind?"

Taking a deep breath, I leaned against the table, searching for the right words amidst the chaos swirling inside me. "It's about the job offer," I began, my heartbeat quickening. "I feel torn between going after this opportunity and staying here, where I've found so much comfort and support." Brody leaned back in his chair, processing my words. "It's a big decision, I know," he said thoughtfully. "What is pulling you toward the big city? Is it ambition or the need for professional validation?" "A bit of both, I think," I admitted, vulnerability washing over me. "I have always wanted to be successful, and this feels like a chance to prove myself. But I also can't shake the feeling that leaving would mean risking everything we have started together." "Ruby, your goals matter," he replied, sincerity grounding his voice. "I'd never want you to sacrifice your dreams for me. But you need to consider what truly makes you happy. Fulfilment comes in many forms."

His words resonated deeply, igniting a flicker of self-awareness within me. I thought of the connections I was forging with Brody, with Ethan, and within myself. It dawned on me that true success was not solely about career highs but about building a meaningful life surrounded by love and support. "Staying for love..." I murmured, contemplating the profound implications behind the sentiment. "It means choosing a deeper ambition, one rooted in relationships rather than titles. Yet can I really leave behind a once-in-a-lifetime chance?" "Ultimately, it's your choice, Ruby," Brody reminded gently, his gaze unwavering. "But whatever you decide, know that I'll be here supporting you and the path you choose." In that moment, I felt an overwhelming sense of gratitude for his support. It became clear to me that no matter which road I travelled, Brody's presence in my life would forever anchor my decisions. But would pursuing love alongside my ambitions even be feasible?

As the waves of contemplation swirled around me, a thought struck, sending ripples of unease through my heart: could our romantic growth withstand the uncertainty of my aspirations? Would I be able to elevate my career without jeopardizing the tenuous bonds I had formed? If I chose to stay, it would require a leap of faith—a commitment to forge a life with Brody that embraced my aspirations without abandoning my dream. My phone buzzed jarring reminder of the impending deadline looming over me. Would this decision lead me to fulfilment, or was it just another diversion from the happiness I had found? "Ruby?" Brody's gentle voice broke through my spiralling thoughts. "Are you okay?" I swallowed hard, forcing myself to focus on the present moment. "I'm just... overwhelmed, Brody. I want to make the right choice, but it feels impossible." He reached out, taking my hand in his. "You don't have to make the decision now," he said softly. "Let the information settle before you jump to a conclusion. Whatever choice you make, we'll work through it together, I promise."

A weight lifted off my shoulders as I met his gaze. I could feel the sincerity in his words resonate deeply within me. "You're right. I don't need to rush this. It's just... it's all so much." Brody nodded in understanding. "Why don't we take a moment to step back from it all? Maybe we can brainstorm some options together—what staying might look like and how I can help you pursue your passions here." Encouraged, I released a breath I didn't realize I was holding. "That sounds good. And maybe I should also think about how I would feel if I accepted the job. What would that look like for us, for our family?" With renewed determination, we shifted our focus from the immediate pressures of the job offer to envisioning a future together. Brody picked up a notepad and began jotting down ideas—how we could expand the outreach program, the adventures we would take as a family, and the intimate moments we cherished.

As we brainstormed, I felt the energy in the room shift; our synergy uncovered new avenues of communication and transparency. Engaging in this exercise allowed me to see how intertwined our lives had become, even as we navigated the uncertainties. "Okay," I smiled, feeling lighter. "Let's list the things I would miss out on if I took the job." As we fleshed out the details in a dialogue thick with appreciation, it became clear that Brody's presence—and our shared moments—held more value than any promotion could offer. Our connection deepened with every exchange; each shared dream illuminated our path ahead. Just when the atmosphere began to feel invigorating, my phone buzzed again, pulling my attention. I glanced down to see a new notification from the hiring manager. Before I could read the message, Brody's phone rang.

"Hold on a second," he said, glancing at the screen, which displayed an unknown number. "I need to take this. It could be work." I nodded and watched him as he stepped away to answer the call. I turned my attention back to my device, anxiety creeping in once more. Curiosity built inside me, but I forced myself to set my phone down. I wanted to stay present in this moment. "Hello?" I heard Brody say, his voice edged with concern. "This is Brody." I couldn't hear the other side of the conversation, but I noticed the tension returning to his posture, the furrow in his brow deepening. He gripped the phone tightly, and I sensed that whatever was being said wasn't good. My thoughts spiralled again, anxiety gnawing at my chest. What if this call changed everything? "Is everything okay?" I asked as Brody ended the call and returned to my side; concern etched deep within his eyes. "We need to talk—now," he said, urgency threading through his tone, stripping away the warmth we had just cultivated. I felt my heart race, fear tightening its grip. "What do you mean? Is it bad?" Brody swallowed hard; lines of worry etched across his face. "There's been significant development regarding the acquisition, and it involves me directly." My heart sank. "What does that mean for us?" I whispered, searching for answers in his eyes. "I don't know," he replied, voice strained. "They might need me to relocate immediately to help oversee a transition. It's about to get complicated, and I don't know how much time I'll have before I must leave." With those words, I felt the walls closing in around me. The uncertain path we had begun to navigate now hung in the balance, poised on the edge of catastrophic change.

"What does that mean for us? You can't just leave, Brody. What about Ethan? What about us?" "I know," he replied, running a hand through his hair, frustration simmering just beneath the surface. "But they're saying the acquisition is at a critical juncture, and they need me on-site to navigate the changes. It's not just about my job; it could affect everything we've been working toward at the outreach program." My heart ached at the thought of him being pulled away from our life together—the life we had begun crafting. "So, what? You'll just pick up and go?" I felt the frustration rising within me, urgency boiling over. "It's not that simple," he said, desperation threading through his voice. "I didn't want this to happen, but I don't have control over what's happening at the company. This could ruin the future I've envisioned for us, both personally and professionally."

A sharp crack echoed through the foundation of our hopes. "What if you go, Brody, and you don't come back? What if I'm left here sorting through my own decisions while your career takes you away?" "Ruby, listen to me," he stepped closer, desperation in his eyes, pleading for my understanding. "I am not leaving, and I want to maintain what we have established together." But if I do not step up when it's needed, I could lose everything, including this opportunity. Everything I've worked for is at stake." His words dug deep, igniting a storm of emotions within me. I wanted to pull him close, to find solace in him, but the fear of uncertainty clouded my heart. "What if they need you for months, Brody? Months away from Ethan and me?" I pressed, my voice trembling. "I don't know!" he admitted, frustration and fear spilling over. "But we need to prepare for that possibility. If it happens, I promise we'll face it together, no matter how hard it gets." The earnestness in his voice tugged at my heart, igniting a flicker of hope amidst the chaos.

Yet, just when I thought I could embrace that feeling, the doorbell chimed again unexpectedly and jarring. "Who could that be?" Brody asked, concern etched in his features. "It's late for visitors." "I have no idea," I replied, my stomach tightening. "I hope it's not more bad news." Brody walked cautiously to the door, his demeanour reflecting the same mixture of anxiety and uncertainty that enveloped me. As he opened it, I held my breath, anxiety flooding my senses. What news awaited us now? When Brody swung the door wide, the figure standing there sent a jolt through me. It was a familiar face—the hiring manager from the big-city job—the one I had just sent my declination email to. "Ruby!" the manager exclaimed, eyes sparkling with excitement and urgency. "I'm glad I caught you. There's been a major development, and I really think you need to hear this."

"What? I don't understand," I stammered, feeling the ground shift beneath me. "I sent my response. I thought that was it." Brody looked from the manager to me, confusion evident on his face. The shift in dynamics was palpable, and the air crackled with the weight of unspoken possibilities. Suddenly, I felt like I was caught in a whirlwind, the decision that had seemed so clear moments ago now splintering into countless paths. "Can we talk?" the manager urged, his eyes gleaming with a mix of excitement and urgency. "I really think you need to hear this in private." Understanding the weight of the moment, I felt a mix of anxiety and curiosity. "Uh, okay," I stammered, stepping aside to let the manager enter our home. "What's this about?" Brody stood at my side, a silent pillar of support, though the tension in his shoulders spoke volumes about his concern. The room felt charged with anticipation as the manager took a seat at the table, motioning for me to do the same. "Ruby, I appreciate your initial response to the job offer, but after some discussions within our leadership team, we've reconsidered your application based on your unique potential and insight," he began, his tone earnest. "We believe you could be the perfect addition to our team, and there's an opportunity that has just opened up—one that aligns better with your skills and gives you more leadership in our projects."

"What do you mean?" I asked, bewildered. "I thought I was no longer being considered after I sent my reply." "We value what you bring to the table, and we still hold you in high regard," the manager explained. "This new role would allow you to lead projects that resonate more with your vision. It's a significant step up in responsibility, a chance to influence our outreach globally, with the backing needed to make a real impact." My heart raced. The very thoughts of ambition that had stirred me earlier now collided with this added information. "Wait, but what does that mean for my decision? I thought I had made it clear that I was choosing to stay here."

ANA MONROY

Brody leaned against the counter, his presence a steadying force, but I could sense the heaviness of his thoughts as well. "Take your time, Ruby," the manager urged, sensing my hesitation. "We understand you have other commitments. But I'm here to offer you a modified offer with a revised timeline for your decision. You'll have a chance to explore the role and see if it is the right fit without the pressure of making an immediate move." "But" I hesitated, glancing at Brody, "What about my life here? My family? The outreach work with Brody and Ethan?" The manager's expression softened. "I understand your hesitation. The opportunity I am presenting isn't about a job; it's about crafting experiences that align with your career ambitions and meaningful social impact. We want to cultivate that connection, allowing you to make a real difference. I have discussed this potential synergy with my team, and we believe that your unique perspective could bring invaluable insights." As his words sank in, I felt my heart race, a flurry of possibilities igniting my imagination. On the one hand, this new opportunity could open the door to a prestigious career I had always dreamed of; on the other, it posed a challenge to the heartfelt life I was constructing with Brody and Ethan. The threads of my existence felt increasingly frayed as I wrestled with the implications of this development, torn between two compelling futures. "Can I have a moment?" I finally managed to say, glancing up at Brody, whose face betrayed a mixture of support and uncertainty.

He was wrestling with his own emotions, and I could sense the weight of this conversation bearing down on him. "Absolutely," he replied, his voice steady yet tinged with concern. He took a step back, creating a small space between us that allowed me the privacy I needed to contemplate the weight of the moment. Once the manager nodded and took a step back as well, I felt the whirlpool of thoughts swirl in my mind, each competing for my attention. Could this potential job align with my pursuit of a meaningful life filled with purpose? How would this decision affect my relationship with Brody and Ethan, the two people who anchored my heart? And could I truly thrive in a demanding role while still nurturing the deep connections that mattered most to me? Taking a deep breath to steady myself, I turned my gaze toward Brody, whose presence felt like an unwavering support.

"What do you think I should do?" I asked softly, searching his eyes for insight—the comfort of our bond grounding me amid uncertainty. Brody stepped closer, locking eyes with me. "I have always believed in your potential, Ruby. It has been evident for as long as I have known you. I want you to explore this opportunity fully, but I also want you to be certain that whatever choice you make reflects who you genuinely want to be. Do you feel this path aligns with what you have been looking for?" Tears brimmed in my eyes as I pondered his words, a surge of emotion washing over me. The enormity of the decisions before me weighed heavily, stirring both excitement and fear. "What changes everything for us?" I murmured, my voice choking on the vulnerability of my thoughts. Brody gently reached for my hand, intertwining our fingers in a gesture that both comforted and inspired me. "No matter what happens, Ruby, I am here for you. I promise I will not let anything come between us.

Together we can adapt to whatever challenges may come our way. Just remember, love can grow and evolve in unexpected ways. Staying true to yourself does not mean you have to sacrifice your happiness or our connection." Just as the gravity of our conversation lingered, the doorbell rang again, pulling us back to the present. My stomach tightened, a mix of curiosity and apprehension flooding my senses. I felt the tide of change shifting around us, leaving me breathless.

"What now?" I whispered, overwhelmed by a wave of anticipation, both excited and anxious at the unexpected interruption. Brody furrowed his brow, glancing toward the door with a cautious expression. "I'll see who it is," he replied, the tension in his voice palpable. As he approached the door, I remained close behind, my heart pounding in my chest. What awaited us now? The thought of yet another development felt like a rollercoaster ride; I was at the peak, suspended in uncertainty, waiting to discover where the next turn might take me. Brody opened the door, and I held my breath, anticipation hanging heavily in the air. At first, I could not see who was there, but as Brody stepped aside, I saw a person standing in the doorway.

My eyes widened in shock—it was none other than the hiring manager from the big-city job I had just previously turned down. "Ruby!" he exclaimed, his expression a mix of excitement and urgency. "I am glad I caught you. There has been a major development, and you need to hear this." "What? But I sent my response," I stammered, bewildered. "I thought that was it." Brody looked between the two of us, his brow furrowing with confusion. The atmosphere shifted dramatically as the weight of the moment pressed down on me. "Can we talk?" the manager urged. "I really think you need to hear this in private." My heart raced as I processed the influx of emotions that bubbled inside me. "Uh, okay," I managed, stepping aside to let him enter our home. Brody, standing at my side, mirrored my concern, and I felt the tension between us as thick as fog.

As the manager made himself comfortable, I could feel the uncertainty of the moment hanging in the air like an uninvited guest. "So, what's this about?" I asked, my voice was steadier than I felt. "Ruby, I appreciate your initial response to the job offer," he began, his tone serious. "After some discussions within our leadership team, we have reconsidered your application based on your unique potential and insight. We believe you could be the perfect addition to our team, and there is an opportunity that has just opened—one that aligns better with your skills and gives you a more substantial leadership role in our projects."

My heart raced at his words, the implications flooding my mind. "What do you mean?" I stammered, bewildered. "I thought my response meant I was no longer in the running." "We value what you bring to the table, and clearly, the team reached a consensus about your potential," he replied. "This new position offers a chance to lead initiatives that resonate deeply with your vision and passion. It is a significant step up, allowing you to influence our outreach on a global scale, making a tangible impact." Suddenly, feelings of excitement clawed at me, battling with the reality of what Brody and I had just discussed. I turned to him, searching for reassurance in his expression.

He stood there, an unwavering pillar, but I could see the storm of emotions brewing beneath the surface. "Wait, but what does this mean for the decision I just made? I thought I chose to stay," I said, my mind racing. "What about my life here? My family? Our work together?" The manager's eyes softened with understanding. "I realize this is a lot to process, but I want to stress that this opportunity is meant to enhance your passion for social impact. You would not have to make an immediate move, and we are more than willing to be flexible with the timeline for your decision." I felt like I was standing on the edge of a precipice, and a hundred thoughts raced through my mind. Could I really take this new opportunity without sacrificing the life I was building here? Would the demands of a high-level job consume me entirely, pulling me away from Brody and Ethan? "Can I have a moment?" I finally said, glancing back at Brody, my partner through so much. I needed to hear his thoughts, even if I was already beginning to sense the answers forming within me. "Take all the time you need," Brody replied quietly, his gaze steady, yet filled with concern. I took a deep breath and moved to the far side of the kitchen, my heart racing. As I weighed my options, the gravity of my decision bore down on me. I knew I was faced with a momentous choice—one that could redefine my career, my relationship, and my sense of self. Taking a moment to gather my emotions, I recalled Brody's earlier words.

He had gently encouraged me to follow my heart, to embrace my dreams—advice that now echoed in my mind. Standing there, I felt a rush of clarity. I could envision paths diverging before me. If I accepted this position, I would be stepping into the spotlight I always craved, but I would also have to navigate the impact it would have on my family.

Conversely, declining it meant finding a deeper kind of success rooted in my love for Brody and Ethan—a choice that also felt powerful and right. Taking another deep breath, I faced Brody, who had stepped closer, waiting patiently. "Brody," I began, my voice steady, "I have been doing a lot of thinking.

I have this opportunity that is more than I ever dreamed of, and it could be everything for which I have worked. But I cannot let that come at the cost of what we have. I do not want to sacrifice us for my ambition, and I do not want you to feel like I am abandoning this life we have built together." His eyes softened as he listened intently. "I want you to chase your dreams, Ruby. You deserve every chance to fulfil your potential. I believe you can pursue it while still maintaining what we have. It does not have to be one or the other."

My heart swelled at his support. I stepped forward, intertwining my fingers with his. "So...what if I ask for some time to decide? Maybe I can explore this opportunity while seeing how I can still be here with you and Ethan. I want to find a way to do both." Brody smiled, relief washing over his features. "That sounds like a plan. Remember, you are not alone in this. We will figure it out together. Whatever choice you make, I want you to be happy, Ruby." A sense of calm settled over me, and I turned back to the manager, who had been waiting patiently. "I appreciate the opportunity you're presenting, and I'd like to understand more about it before making any decisions."

"Of course! Let us outline the details and see how we can make it work for you while giving you the room you need to decide." As the three of us delved into discussions about the role, potential projects, and timelines, I felt the tension in my heart gradually ease. The path ahead began to reveal itself more clearly. I could explore this new role while simultaneously nurturing the relationship I held dear, weaving together the threads of my professional aspirations and personal connections.

That evening, as I sat with Brody and Ethan at the dining table, sharing a simple dinner, I felt a mixture of excitement and relief wash over me. The conversation flowed easily, laughter punctuating the air as we shared stories and made plans for the weekend. With each passing moment, I realized how deeply rooted I was in this life—the warmth of our home, the bond we were building, and the vibrancy of our shared dreams. After dinner, I found myself drawn to the window again, watching as the stars began to dot the sky. It was here, in this moment of stillness, that I could feel the conflicting paths I stood before reconcile into one. I knew I had the chance to pursue the ambitious career I had always desired while simultaneously nurturing the love and life I held dear. "Ruby?" Brody's voice broke through my thoughts, grounding me. He came up beside me, placing a gentle hand on my shoulder. "What's going on in that beautiful mind of yours?" "I was just thinking about everything," I said, turning to face him, reflecting the honesty in my heart. "About what this new opportunity could mean, and how I want to make it work alongside our life together."

He smiled softly; his eyes filled with warmth. "You do not have to have all the answers tonight. Just know that whatever path you choose, we are in this together." As a sense of peace settled over me, I leaned into Brody, feeling the steadiness of his presence soothe my worries. "I am going to think about everything carefully. I want to make sure I am making the right choice, not just for my career, but for us—for our family."

"Take your time, Ruby. You know what you are capable of. Trust yourself," he urged, his voice a soothing balm to my uncertainties. "Thank you, Brody. For everything." I let a smile slip through, feeling bolstered by his unwavering support. Our moment was interrupted when Ethan bounced into the room, a drawing in his hand. "Look what I made!" he exclaimed, his eyes wide with excitement. "Wow! That is amazing, buddy! What is it?" I crouched down to examine his artwork. "It's our family!" he said proudly, pointing to stick figures that, despite their simplicity, captured the essence of our bond. I felt my heart swell again, filled with gratitude for this family and the life we were building together.

As I looked at the drawing, a new sense of clarity washed over me. The picture represented everything I valued: my dreams and aspirations, the laughter we shared, and the deep connections between us. The choice I had to make did not have to mean abandoning one for the other; I could sculpt a future that embraced both. As the night wore on, I reflected on everything that had transpired, the weight of my decisions began to feel lighter. I could feel ambition stirring within me, ready to take on the challenges ahead, while still holding tightly to the love that defined me. It was a beautiful balance worth pursuing. With the warm laughter of my family ringing in my ears, I felt resolute. I knew I was ready to embrace whatever came next, to seize both the opportunity before me and the love I so cherished. No matter the outcome, I trusted that I could make this work—both my career and my heart. And with that thought, I smiled, knowing that my life was unfolding in ways I had never imagined, full of potential and promise. The journey ahead was uncertain, but with Brody and Ethan by my side, I felt equipped to face it all. The dream of an ambitious career intertwined with the reality of my beautiful family felt possible, illuminating the path I would choose.

10

Personal Realizations

As Brody stood at the window of his home office, sunlight streaming through the glass and casting warm hues across the room. Leaning against the sill, he breathed in the peaceful sounds of neighbourhood life outside—kids laughing, distant chatter, and the welcoming rustle of leaves. It felt like an idyllic scene, a stark contrast to the swirling chaos within him. He could not shake the profound changes that had begun to unfurl in his life since I had entered it. My presence breathed new life into his home, igniting long-dormant passions and ambitions. As he reflected on his own journey, it became increasingly clear how important my contributions were—not just to our personal lives, but also to his professional aspirations.

The outreach program we had nurtured together had taken root, thriving on the adaptive strategies he had implemented in the business. Yet, this growth felt incomplete without acknowledging my role as a catalyst. I was the bridge connecting his previously isolated career goals to something far grander.

A swell of gratitude washed over him at the thought of her unwavering support and the dynamic energy I brought into our partnership. If only he could do more to support me through my own journey, he mused, realizing that providing consistent spaces for my contributions would not only benefit shared goals between us but also affirm our own bond. My work inspired him to embrace his vulnerabilities, to lean into the beauty of collaboration. With a sense of determination, he began to contemplate the possibility of merging our interests fully.

ANA MONROY

What if we formalized our partnership, combining our talents in a way that elevated us both? The idea sparked a new fire within Brody, igniting the conviction that such a union could propel us to new heights, both personally and professionally. Imagining these scenarios made him resolve and strengthen, ushering in the clarity he desperately needed.

As he returned to his desk, energized by the possibilities, he rifled through notes and sketches. And he envisioned all the ways we could work together, expanding community engagement initiatives, harmonizing our professional goals with the outreach program, and even creating a platform where our combined expertise could shine. Each idea fuelled his excitement, and he felt an exhilarating sense of purpose building within him. Yet, he also recognized the weight of my internal conflicts. My hesitation regarding the job offer hung heavily, a tension that both grounded and distracted me. Would I see the potential in our partnership as he did? Would I recognize that I didn't have to sacrifice my dreams for our relationship, but could we instead weave them together to create something even more powerful?

As he prepared to unveil this vision to me, a sense of urgency rushed over him. He knew he had to approach the conversation with sensitivity. This was not just about a new business direction; it was about solidifying our bond in a way that resonated with both our dreams. The stakes felt high, and he wanted to ensure I understood the depth of his commitment—not just to his goals, but to our future together.

Just then, the ringing of his phone broke his reverie. Glancing at the screen, he saw it was the hiring manager, the very person I had been deliberating over. A flicker of anxiety darted through him. What news awaited us now? Was this call an opportunity or a disruption? Taking a deep breath to centre himself, he answered the phone. "Hello?" "Brody, I'm glad I caught you," the manager said, urgency lacing his voice. "I've just spoken to Ruby, and we need to discuss some critical developments regarding her offer."

The words struck at me like a bolt of lightning, and anticipation gripped me tight. "What do you mean? What is happening?" "The company is shifting directions, and we believe Ruby's insights and talents are even more vital now than we initially realized. I want to discuss how we can structure a role for her that aligns with both her ambitions and the emerging vision of the company. This could open new avenues that benefit both your outreach initiatives and her professional journey." As the conversation unfolded, a rush of excitement filled me, tempered by concern. This could be the moment he had been waiting for—a chance to formalize our ambitions into a collaborative venture that would amplify their growth. Yet the weight of the decision still loomed large.

He knew I would need time and support to process whatever changes lay ahead for us. After ending the call, he stood still, the weight of possibility heavy on his shoulders. He recognized a change in basic assumptions unfolding within him—one that embraced the idea of merging our lives—both personally and professionally. With new hope igniting within him, he prepared his thoughts, ready to share this vision with me, eager to unveil the possibilities of our shared future. He walked towards the living area; he could feel the electric energy of what we could build together crackling in the air. Would I share his excitement? Would I seize the chance to redefine not just my career but also our lives together?

Stepping into the living area, he found me seated on the couch, my expression a blend of contemplation and uncertainty. The weight of our earlier conversation still hung in the air between us, thick with significance. He could sense that I was still wrestling with my thoughts, contemplating the implications of the job offer and what it meant for my future. "Hey," I said softly, trying to convey my unwavering support as he sat beside me. "I just got off the phone with the hiring manager. They want to discuss some important developments regarding your offer." My eyes widened slightly, a flicker of curiosity igniting my expression. "What do you mean? What is happening?"

"I think you should hear this," he replied, leaning in closer. "They are shifting direction and believe your insights and talents are more crucial now than they originally thought. There is a possibility for a role that could align perfectly with your ambitions and the outreach initiative we have been cultivating together." he watched as my brow furrowed, processing the news. "An opportunity that aligns with what we're doing here?" I asked tentatively. "But I do not know, Brody. It feels like a lot is changing all at once." "I understand," he said earnestly, feeling the energy of our shared vision pulse between us. "This could be a chance for us to really unite our aspirations—to merge your career goals with the outreach work we have been building. You could lead important projects, making a real difference while still being part of my life here."

Her expression flickered, the gears obviously turning in her mind. "But what if I get caught up in the corporate world again? What if this opportunity changes everything we have been trying to establish together?" "Change can be daunting," he reassured me, squeezing my hand gently. "But it can also bring growth. You have the potential to shape your role in ways that truly reflect who you are. You would not be doing this alone; we would be navigating these waters together." He paused, allowing his words to resonate. "You already have a solid foundation with Ethan and me. Let us make this partnership work for both of us. This could be an opportunity to amplify everything we have built—the love, the outreach program, your passions. I want you to thrive, and I will be right there beside you."

When he spoke, he could see the hesitation still warring in my heart, but there was also a spark of hope beginning to light in my eyes. "You really believe that don't you? That we can make this partnership work?" "I do, more than anything," he confessed, his heart racing. "I want to formalize our dreams together, and I honestly believe we both deserve to thrive, both at home and in our careers. What you do now can serve a larger purpose, and so can I." From that moment, a sense of calm began to settle between us, and the doorbell rang again. And he felt a sudden sense of foreboding rush over him, remembering the interruptions they had faced earlier.

"Who could that be now?" I asked, my voice filled with a mix of curiosity and unease. "Do you want me to get it?" I offered my protective instincts kicking in. "No, I'll check," he said, rising from the couch. The tension in the room had ramped up again, and he wanted to be sure whatever was behind that door would not divert our focus from the discussion we were having. As he opened the door, his heart dropped. Standing before him was a figure he had not expected to see—an old business associate from a past project, someone he thought he had left behind for good.

"Brody," he said with urgency, his expression serious. "We need to talk. It's about the acquisition—there are things you need to know that could change everything." The words sent a shiver down his spine, and he felt an unsettling tension in the pit of his stomach. "What do you mean?" He pressed the anxiety building within him. "There are corporate espionage concerns and a hostile takeover attempt," he explained, and he could feel the gravity of his words weighing heavily in the air. "Your name has come up in conversations, and I came to warn you. If you decide to go ahead with this partnership, you could find yourself caught in a much larger game than you anticipated." I stepped closer, my worry evident in my wide eyes. "Brody, what does this mean for us?" "I need to evaluate my options," he thought aloud, but the discussions with me just moments ago floated back into his mind. They had been talking about merging their lives and aspirations, about building something together, and now this unexpected revelation threatened to unravel those plans. Brody, you must be careful. What if this jeopardizes everything for which we have worked? What if I lose you… or worse? My heart raced as he tried to remain composed. "I'm not abandoning you," he insisted, trying to quell the rising anxiety in the room. "I am not about to let this take away what we have built together. But if I do not step up when it is needed, I could lose everything, including this chance to secure our future."

My gaze bore into mine, my concern palpable. "What if they need you for months, Brody? Months away from me and Ethan?" "I don't know," he admitted, frustration creeping into his voice. "But this acquisition is serious. If they need me on-site to manage the transition, I cannot afford to risk everything. We need to prepare for that possibility, even if it means making tough decisions." The sincerity of his words seemed to hang in the air, heavy with the weight of uncertainty. Just as he was about to continue, a sudden knock at the door drew my attention once more. He glanced at me, a flicker of worry crossing his face, and he took a deep breath before turning back to face the door. "Let me manage this," he said, trying to portray confidence even as anxiety knotted in his stomach. He opened the door cautiously, revealing a familiar face from a different chapter of his past—an old co-worker who had not been in touch for years. As he looked at me, my expression reflected both determination and resilience. He knew that even amid the uncertainty swirling around us, they could forge a path forward if we remained united in our commitment to each other. The weight of the conversation lingered, but now he felt a renewed sense of purpose. The future remained unclear, filled with obstacles and challenges. However, with me and his co-workers' support, he was ready to face whatever came next. Together, we would find a way to navigate this tangled web of opportunity and intrigue, determined to secure our shared dreams and protect the love we had fostered. "Let's get to work," he said, embracing the necessity of action. The events of the day had not unsettled him so much as fuelled a fire to forge our path into the unknown—together.

As he stepped back into the living area with me at his side, what had once felt like a crushing weight on his shoulders now transformed into a collective resolve—an understanding that together we could face whatever challenges lay ahead. He could see that the concern in my eyes was mingled with determination, and that gave him strength. "Let's gather our thoughts and make a plan," he suggested, pulling out a notepad. "We need to be proactive about this, especially since everything feels so unpredictable."

I nodded, my expression shifting from worry to focus. "I agree. It is time to confront these challenges head-on. What do you think our first step should be?" he glanced at the former co-worker, who had taken a seat and was leaning forward in interest. "I think reaching out to those trusted contacts, as you suggested, would be a great start," he replied. "We need to understand the landscape we are navigating. Then we can assess our options more clearly." "Absolutely," I added, my mind clearly working through the strategy. "And we should consider how we can engage the community in this process. If we are dealing with corporate espionage, being transparent and building goodwill might serve us well." "Yes, yes! That is perfect," I said, feeling an exhilarating rush of collaboration. "We can leverage our outreach strategies to reinforce our standing in the community while managing these corporate threats."

With each idea we collaborated on, the constructive collaboration between me and him felt stronger, and he could sense a unity that we could build upon. The fear that had gripped him earlier began to dissolve, replaced by a sense of shared purpose. As we mapped out our plan, the atmosphere shifted—what had started as uncertainty was now filled with potential. "We'll face this together," he reminded me, looking into my eyes. "No matter what happens, I'm here for you, just as you've always been for me."

The doorbell rang one more time, and instead of dreading, he felt a spark of anticipation. "Let me get it," he said, curious who else might join us in this newfound momentum. He opened the door to find a familiar face—one of their close community contacts who was heavily involved with their outreach program. "Hey, I heard about the acquisition and wanted to check in," they said, their expression earnest. "Come in! You are just in time," he exclaimed, inviting them inside. "We need your perspective on some developments and how we can tackle what's ahead." As his co-worker entered, he saw my eyes light up. The sense of community and support around them felt electric.

Together, they would forge a response that combined our resources, ambitions, and strengths. In that moment, enveloped by the warmth of shared purpose, he felt an overwhelming wave of confidence wash over him. Whatever challenges lay ahead—corporate threats or personal uncertainties—we had the tools to face them together. He turned back to look at me, my smile mirrored his own determination.

The path was still unclear, but one thing was certain: we were stepping boldly forward, ready to create a future woven together by our dreams, love, and the steadfast commitment to one another. The community contact settled into the living area, the energy in the room transformed once again. The air was electric with possibilities. The community worker quickly briefed us on the latest developments regarding the acquisition and the pressing concerns we would have to face.

"I'm glad you're here," he said, feeling a sense of camaraderie as we shared the urgent context of the situation. "We've got a lot on our plates, and your insights could really help us formulate a strategy that not only protects what we've built but also amplifies our outreach efforts." I nodded, my brow furrowing with concentration. "I've had some conversations with other community leaders, and I think we could leverage those relationships to create a unified front," I suggested. "If there's a threat of a corporate takeover, aligning our voices and initiatives could help us maintain community trust and support." "Yes! That would be a crucial move," I interjected enthusiastically. "If we can position our outreach program as a vital community resource, it might rally support against any negative impacts from the acquisition."

With each shared idea, I began to piece together a robust plan, brainstorming about potential events, collaborative projects, and public relations strategies that would help solidify support from the community. The constructive collaboration of our discussion sparked a fire of inspiration in him, rejuvenating the vision of what their outreach programme could accomplish. As he took notes and contributed suggestions, he could not help but glance at me once more. He loved how my passion illuminated the room, and every time I spoke, he felt even more confident in our mission together. Their partnership was growing, becoming something deeply intertwined—both meaningful personally and impactful professionally. The conversation flowed seamlessly, we considered organizing a community event to foster awareness about the acquisition while promoting the outreach initiatives, I could see Brody's eyes shining with excitement. There was undeniable magic in how our dreams were beginning to align, contributing to a shared purpose that felt incredibly powerful. After hours of collaboration, we outlined the next steps before the community contact left.

I felt a buoyancy within Brody that had not been seen before—a clarity and direction he had long craved. "Can you believe how far we've come today?" he asked me as he cleared coffee mugs from the table. "Honestly, it feels almost surreal," I replied, my smile radiant. "I was so nervous about the job offer this morning, but now I feel like we have a real chance to carve out something special—not just for us but for the community too." He nodded, feeling a warm sense of pride swelling in his chest. "And we did it together. I hope you see that your role is just as vital as mine in this. You bring so much to the table—your ideas, your passion, your heart. It is powerful." My eyes sparkled with gratitude as I looked at him. "Thank you for believing In me, Brody. It means everything. I cannot imagine navigating this without your support." Soon after we finished tidying up, I felt a new bond solidify between us.

Our earlier conversations about the future were no longer just theoretical; they were unfolding right before our eyes. They were not just facing the unknown; they were actively shaping it. Once the kitchen was clean, we settled onto the couch, the soft glow of the evening light casting a warm ambiance around us. He took my hand in his, feeling the comfort of their connection. "As we move forward," he began, "I want you to know that whatever the outcome of the acquisition is, we will manage it together. I am committed to our partnership, and I believe in everything we can achieve together." I squeezed his hand tightly, my expression earnest. "And I believe in us too, Brody. This journey might have uncertainties, but I know that with you by my side, we can navigate anything." We shared a quiet moment of understanding, the bond of our love and shared purpose intertwining with our aspirations. He leaned in and kissed my forehead gently, grateful that with every challenge, we kept drawing closer together instead of apart. Just as our conversation turned to planning the next steps, the doorbell rang once more. A smile crept across his face—every sound and development filled him with both intrigue and anticipation.

"Who is it this time?" I asked, raising an eyebrow, half-amused at the unpredictable cascade of visitors. "I'll check," he said, standing up with an eagerness that had come to define this day of unexpected developments. Opening the door, he was greeted by Ethan, his son, bursting with excitement. "Dad! Auntie! You must see this! I made something incredible!" He felt the warmth of joy surge through him. "What is it, buddy?" He asked, his heart swelling as he crouched down to his level. Ethan held up a colourful poster he had made, decorated with drawings of superheroes and our family engaged in activities—painted in bright colours. "It's our family superhero team!" he exclaimed, his eyes wide with enthusiasm. "And you and Ruby are the leading heroes because you help everyone!"

He could not help but smile, beaming with pride at his creativity and the thoughtful homage he was giving to both me and Brody. "I love it! We are the superhero team!" he declared, drawing him into a hug with Ethan. I moved closer to them kneeling beside them, my expression radiant with happiness as I examined Ethan's masterpiece. "This is amazing, Ethan! You have a real talent for art. We should hang this up where everyone can see it!" "Yeah! Right in the living room!" Ethan replied, practically bouncing with excitement. As Brody looked at him, he then realized how beautifully everything fit together—the precious time he spent with his son, 66trugglees and triumphs we shared as a family, our love, and now the opportunity to work together on something that could change our future for the better. He felt a surge of gratitude caught up in the moment—the simplicity of his family, the laughter and love that enveloped us, and the dreams to be nurtured together. "Tonight, let's celebrate," he said, standing up and straightening. "How about we make a special dinner together? We can even create our own superhero-themed outfits!" "Yay! Super dinners!" Ethan shouted, raising his arms in joy.

"Alright, superhero team," I said, standing up with them and taking charge. "Let us whip up something amazing! But first, we will need to figure out our superhero names." We moved outside the office, laughter and joy replaced the earlier tension. The urgency of the external threats faded into the background as we rallied together, ready to face whatever came next. The plans for the outreach initiatives, the discussions surrounding my job offer, and the looming corporate challenges became just a small part of a much larger tapestry—a tapestry woven with love, adventure, and strong family bonds.

We worked side by side in the office, Brody realized that the decisions ahead, no matter how daunting, were steps on a journey that we would undertake together. Whether it involved navigating the corporate responsibilities, and my career aspirations, or the commitments we made to each other and to Ethan, he knew we could tackle it all. The evening unfolded like a scene from one of Ethan's imaginative stories—a whirlwind of activity punctuated by laughter, superhero banter, but the plans to cook dinner back at home, was looming over the horizon that afternoon. With every hour passing by, he felt the unshakeable certainty that this was his true path. And so, as the sun dipped below the horizon with the twilight sky enveloping the world outside, the journey back home filled Brody and me with bright colours of laughter and love. Brody knew that whatever challenges lay ahead, we would face them as a united front, the superhero team we always been destined to become.

11

ANA MONROY
Forging Forward

I stood in the warm glow of Brody's living room, feeling a renewed sense of purpose as I watched him flip through his business strategy documents. Despite the fears that sometimes creased his brow, I could sense a flicker of determination reigniting within him. With every word exchanged and every challenge we confronted together, my unwavering presence only strengthened his resolve. "Brody, you have incredible potential within you," I said softly, leaning over the table to help him sort through his ideas. "You have built something remarkable already.

You just need to embrace this next stage of your journey." He looked up, uncertainty still shadowing his features. "It is just...what if I fail at this? What if stepping out of my comfort zone leads to more challenges?" I smiled and reached out to touch his hand gently. "Every growth comes with its challenges, but that is where the real magic happens. We learn from those moments, and they shape us into stronger versions of ourselves." As I watched him, I could see his expression beginning to shift, the weight of my words sinking in. There was something about my conviction that inspired confidence in him, awakening a sense of determination he had almost forgotten. "You really believe that?" he asked, his voice steadying. "I do," I affirmed, feeling a warmth spread through me. "And that is why I think it's time for you to officially rebrand your business strategy. You need to incorporate growth goals that highlight your values and aspirations. We can do this together; I know we can!"

While we worked through the ideas, I could feel my enthusiasm becoming contagious. Cozy evenings spent in the warmth of his home turned into productive brainstorming sessions, filled with laughter and personal anecdotes that intertwined our lives and ambitions seamlessly. Each conversation blurred the boundaries that had once existed between our professional and personal aspirations.

I cherished these moments—the way we navigated challenges and shared our hopes and dreams. Brody was not just listening to my ideas; he was actively engaging with them, integrating my insights to shape a forward-thinking vision for his business. It was invigorating to witness this evolution. "I never thought about using those elements," he admitted one evening as we reviewed marketing strategies. "Your perspective is opening doors I didn't know existed." "Together, we can forge a path that reflects who you really are and what you want to create," I replied, my heart fluttering with anticipation for the future we could build as a team. Our connection deepened with every discussion, and I began to feel that we were moving beyond mere colleagues or acquaintances—we were becoming allies united in purpose. Then, as we continued brainstorming ways to incorporate our passions into a unified vision, Brody paused, looking contemplative. "What if we merged our aspirations, not just professionally, but personally too?" he suggested playfully, a teasing glint in his eyes.

My heart skipped a beat at the implication of his suggestion. "Brody, are you serious?" I asked, a mix of surprise and excitement flooding through me. "You're talking about blending our dreams into something more significant?" "I think we can navigate this journey together, evolving our lives in a way that encompasses both our dreams," he replied earnestly. "We could create something truly unique, something that honours both of our ambitions." The weight of his words vibrated in my chest, teasing ideas of what our future might hold—one where our lives were intertwined in more meaningful ways. But just as my excitement bubbled within me, a nagging doubt lingered in the corners of my mind. Was I ready to explore the depths of this new partnership and everything it might signify?

Before I could delve deep into my thoughts, the doorbell rang loudly, disrupting our intimate moment and leaving us caught between the tranquillity of our planning and the unpredictability of what awaited us outside. "Who could that be?" I wondered aloud, my heart racing again as I instinctively glanced toward Brody, sensing another disruption to our evening. "I'll check," he said, moving toward the door with determination. As he opened it, the welcoming glow of our home illuminated the doorway, but anticipation filled the air with electric tension. What would this visitor bring—good news or further complications, reshaping the promising path we were forging together? When Brody opened the door, I held my breath, anticipation weighing heavily in the air. Standing there was an old business associate of Brody's, her expression a mix of urgency and excitement. "Brody! I hope I'm not interrupting," she stepped inside without waiting for an invitation. "I just received some insightful information regarding the acquisition that I thought you'd want to hear."

My heart sank. I stood nearby, feeling a mix of curiosity and anxiety as I glanced at Brody and the unexpected visitor. "What kind of information?" I asked, sensing the familiar knot tighten in my stomach. "There have been some positive developments," the visitor explained, her eyes gleaming. "Positive developments?" Brody echoed, his eyebrows lifting in surprise. "What do you mean?" The visitor took a closer step, her tone urgent yet excited. "The company is committed to expanding and wants you on board to help lead some major new initiatives. They recognize the potential you bring to the table, especially your emphasis on community engagement." A rush of excitement coursed through me as I watched Brody's eyes light up. "Really? That is incredible news!" he exclaimed, an infectious smile breaking across his face. "But there's more," she continued, her expression becoming serious. "There will be significant changes in leadership and how roles will be defined moving forward. You need to decide quickly if this is a direction you want to pursue, as the competition is already moving to secure key positions within the company." I exchanged a glance with Brody, my heart racing. This was exactly the kind of opportunity we had hoped for, but it came with the prospect of upheaval and uncertainty. Would this development pull us apart or draw us closer together? "Brody, are you okay with this?" I asked softly, trying to gauge his feelings about the good news.

"Honestly? I am thrilled," he replied, excitement radiating from him. "This could be a meaningful change for me—and for us. But... I want to make sure we approach it thoughtfully. I do not want to ignore how it impacts our plans." The urgency of the moment intensified, and warmth and pride swell within me at Brody's commitment to our partnership. "We can work through the details together, just like we've been doing," I reassured him. "We can figure out how this aligns with our goals and with Ethan's needs." As the conversation continued, we discussed how this potential new role for Brody could align with our outreach initiatives. Excitement coursed through me, tempered with the need for caution. "This is an incredible opportunity for you, Brody, but I'm still worried about how it impacts all of us," I admitted. "Ruby, I truly believe this is a chance for us to unite our aspirations," he said, his expression earnest. "We could integrate your passions into this vision. I want this to be something we build together—both professionally and personally." The weight of his suggestions began to resonate within me. Suddenly, the idea of a partnership that blended our lives and careers appeared tangible, accessible. "Could we really? Could I go after my dreams without sacrificing our life together?" "Absolutely," he affirmed, his confidence buoying my spirits. "This is about being partners in every sense. We support one another's goals while defining a shared future. Just then, the doorbell rang again, unexpectedly. I felt my stomach tighten with a mixture of apprehension and anticipation. "What now?" I whispered, looking at Brody, who seemed equally surprised.

ANA MONROY

"I'll get it," he offered, moving toward the door as I remained firmly rooted by the couch, my heart pounding. When he opened the door, I could see him stiffen for a moment. I could not see who it was, but I sensed the tension pouring into the room, thickening the air. "Brody," I heard a familiar voice say, and my heart dropped as I recognized it. My old colleague stood there, and I knew from the way she shifted uncomfortably that she was serious. "We need to talk."

Panic flooded through me as I exchanged glances with Brody. Just as things seemed to be aligning, this familiar face could bring a whirlwind. "Can it wait?" Brody replied, a note of defensiveness in his tone. "We're in the middle of something important." "It can't," she insisted, stepping inside without waiting for an invitation. "This is about your career and Ruby's future as well. You both need to know what is at stake." The tension in the room grew thicker than before. I felt the weight of uncertainty press down on my chest. "What do you mean?" I asked, my voice barely above a whisper. "They're moving fast with the acquisition, and I heard some concerning things about the leadership changes I think you should know. It is going to shake up everything you are planning for the outreach initiatives."

I absorbed her words; worry knotted my stomach. I had just begun to see the potential! Who knew how these new developments would affect our plans and whether I would keep my footing as Brody navigated this unpredictable landscape? "Please, sit down," Brody said firmly, motioning to the couch. "This sounds serious." As she settled into the chair opposite us, I felt a mixture of dread and anticipation.

The future I had begun to envision felt precarious, and yet I could not ignore the flicker of hope that remained alive in the heart of our conversation. As we prepared to discuss whatever lay ahead, I reminded myself that, no matter what the outcome, we were in this together. The tension in the room was palpable as we settled into the living area, the weight of the moment crashing down around us. I could feel my heart racing as I looked at Brody, who leaned forward, an intent expression on his face.

"Okay, let's hear what you have to say," he urged, his tone steady despite the storm of emotions swirling behind his eyes. The visitor took a deep breath before speaking. "As I mentioned, there are rapid changes happening within the company. I've heard there are plans for significant restructuring, and it is likely going to lead to some intense shifts in leadership." She glanced between us, gauging our reactions. My stomach twisted at the implications. "What does that mean for Brody's role and the outreach initiatives we've been discussing?" I pressed, desperate for clarity. "It means you both need to be prepared for some major upheaval," she said, a serious note in her voice.

"Brody, your name has been mentioned as a key player in the new direction the company wants to take. However, these discussions are happening quickly, and the new leadership could impact everything you have built together." Brody shifted slightly and his anxiety was clear in his posture. "What kind of upheaval are we talking about? Is my position at risk?" "It's not about risk per se, but change is coming," she explained. "New leaders mean new priorities—a shift in focus that may not align with your outreach goals. If you want to solidify your role, you will need to act fast and make your intentions clear. And Ruby, they will expect you to come along if Brody decides to take their new offer." The news hit me like a ton of bricks. I was about to decide about my future, but now I need to consider Brody's choices as well. Could I really step back and sacrifice my professional ambitions for the sake of supporting his career? "Do you really think I should take this opportunity?" Brody asked, turning to the visitor, his eyes searching for guidance. "If it means a complete rework of our plans, I don't want to jeopardize what Ruby, and I have built." She looked thoughtful, clearly weighing her words.

"Brody, if you articulate a sharp vision for your outreach initiatives and how they align with the company's new direction, you could be a powerful advocate for both your goals and Ruby's passions. It is about framing this as a partnership, not just a job for you." I exchanged a glance with Brody, feeling the intensity of our shared concerns. The prospect of him moving forward in his career was exhilarating, but I could not shake the fear of losing the connection we had established.

"What if we lose sight of our family in all this?" I said quietly, my voice tinged with worry. "What if this 'new direction' pulls us apart instead of bringing us closer together?" Brody wrapped an arm around my shoulders, pulling me in close. "We can navigate this together, Ruby. We'll find a way to integrate our ambitions while nurturing the life we are building.

If this opportunity allows us to advance our outreach goals, it is worth considering. But we must be honest about our priorities." "Exactly," the visitor added, her expression softening. "This can be a chance to strengthen your partnership, but it'll take clear communication and a commitment to aligning your personal and professional lives." As the weight of their words settled in, I began to see a glimmer of what could be—a unified vision that incorporated both our dreams and aspirations. But I also knew that navigating this new terrain would not be easy; it would require vulnerability and trust. "What would that look like?" I asked, trying to imagine our lives melded with this potential career path while still holding onto what mattered most. "How can we maintain our family focus while embracing your career changes?" Brody leaned forward, his eyes lighting up with determination. "We will develop a shared strategy that emphasizes our values as a family while pursuing our respective goals. We will draw on our strengths to forge ahead, both in our personal lives and our professional endeavours. If we come together as partners, we can elevate each other.

I felt hopeful realizing that with open communication and a willingness to adapt, we could navigate this unpredictable landscape together. The excitement I felt for Brody's ambitions began to meld with my own aspirations, creating a sense of cohesion that I hadn't anticipated. Just then, the doorbell rang once more, and I felt my heart jump. "Another interruption?" I murmured, glancing at Brody. He seemed aware of my apprehension but nodded determination, ready to face whatever awaited us. "I'll get it this time," he said, moving toward the door.

As the door creaked open, my mind raced with possibilities about what would come through next. But as Brody opened it, I was quickly greeted with a familiar face—one I had not seen in a long time. It was Jessica, Brody's ex-wife. She stood at the threshold, her expression a mix of determination and urgency. "Brody," she said, her voice steady but firm. "We need to talk about Ethan."

Instantly, I could feel the tension rise in the room. Brody's demeanour shifted, and instinctively I stepped closer, ready to support him in whatever unfolding drama was about to occur. Jessica," Brody replied, surprised. "What's going on?" "It's important," she insisted, pushing the door open slightly as if to stress the urgency. "Ethan needs to be prepared for some changes that might affect him. I have heard about the acquisition, and I want to discuss how it could impact our arrangements." I felt my heart begin to race, the earlier discussions about opportunities and dreams veering dangerously close to the chaotic reality of co-parenting and the complications that came with it. "Brody, should we let her in?" I asked quietly, unsure of how to navigate this sudden shift in the conversation. "Yeah, let's talk," he said, stepping back and inviting Jessica inside. "But we need to be careful here. This is not about us anymore; it is about Ethan."

As she entered, I could sense the gravity of the situation weighing down on us. I watched the dynamics shift as she settled into the living room. Brody and Jessica had a shared history, and I could feel that old tension that occasionally arose when they were together. "What kind of impact are you talking about?" Brody asked, his tone apprehensive. "I know things are changing with your job, and I'm aware of the stress of making those kinds of decisions," Jessica replied, her voice steady.

"But we need to make sure that Ethan is not caught in the crossfire. I want him to feel secure, especially with everything that is happening." Her concern for Ethan was genuine, and I admired her for that. Still, I could not shake the feeling of unease that crept through me. This conversation could easily spiral, pulling us all into a whirlwind of unresolved issues. "Ethan is our priority," Brody said defensively, his focus shifting to me. "I'm not going to let any changes—whether from work or personal life—affect him negatively."

"I know," Jessica replied, raising her hands slightly as if to calm him. "I am not trying to undermine your plans. I just want to ensure that his emotional needs are met. You know how kids can notice tension." The conversation hung in the air, charged with emotion. Brody glanced at me, silently seeking support as he navigated the complexities of co-parenting while managing the potential upheaval at work. "We were just talking about how to integrate our work together and make sure Ethan feels secure in our family," I interjected gently. "We want to thrive both at home and in our careers, and I believe communication is key for all of us." Jessica seemed to soften slightly, her eyes flickering with realization. "I understand. And I want that for him too. I just thought it would be important to discuss how the changes affect our arrangements and if there is any way, we can work together to support him."

"I appreciate you bringing this up," Brody said carefully. "We want to do what is best for Ethan, and I am glad we can have these conversations. It is important for all of us to stay aligned, especially with everything changing." Jessica nodded, and for a moment, I could see the three of us sitting down together, working as a team for Ethan's benefit. As conflicting emotions swirled within me—fear, hope, anxiety, possibility—I realized that this was an opportunity to reinforce the bonds between us. "Let's create a plan that works for all of us," I proposed, my voice steady. "We will consider each other's needs—yours, Brody's, and Ethan's. We can schedule regular check-ins, especially now that things are shifting."

Brody's expression softened, and he was clearly appreciative. "Yes! That sounds excellent. Communication will keep everything on track." Jessica agreed, and we spent the next few minutes discussing how to navigate Ethan's emotional needs, ensuring a united front while approaching any upcoming changes with care. The conversation continued, and I felt my resolve strengthened. Even if my future with Brody seemed unclear, one truth remained constant: we could face anything together, as long as we communicated openly and supported each other. With a plan forming and a sense of collaboration growing, I looked at Brody and Jessica, realizing how interconnected our lives had become. While challenges were inevitable, so too was our commitment to create a nurturing environment for Ethan—one built on love, transparency, and shared dreams.

Finally, with the discussion wrapping up, I felt hopeful about what lay ahead. Brody and I felt hopeful about what lay ahead. Brody and I would work on our future while ensuring that Ethan felt secure during the changes surrounding him. The evening had transformed from one of uncertainty into a collaborative effort, a reminder that we could thrive together even amid external pressures. As we concluded our discussions, I saw the tension in Brody's shoulders ease. "Thank you for being open to this," he said, looking at Jessica. "We really need to keep the lines of communication clear for Ethan's sake. It means a lot to us." "Absolutely," Jessica replied, her voice genuine. "I want to ensure he feels supported during what could be a confusing time." She glanced at me, a flicker of understanding between us. "And I appreciate both of you for prioritizing him."

Once Jessica left, I turned to Brody, who stood by the door, a small smile breaking free. "That went better than expected," I observed, my relief palpable. "I think we're starting to find the right balance." "Yeah," he replied, moving closer to me. "I am glad we could address those worries together. It just reinforces how important our partnership is—not just in business, but as co-parents too." I stepped into his embrace, feeling the warmth and strength radiate from him. "I am so grateful for your support, Brody. I can sense we are creating something special here." "Together," he said, pulling back to look at me, his eyes filled with sincerity. "No matter what happens with my job or our plans, we will figure it out together. We will forge a path that honours our dreams while always keeping Ethan at the centre."

With his words echoing in my mind, a surge of determination filled me. I knew we faced challenges ahead, but with this united front, I was confident we could navigate anything that came our way. As we moved back to the living area, I caught a glimpse of Ethan's superhero artwork hanging on the wall, and it struck me just how intertwined our lives had become. It was not just about business goals or career aspirations; it was about building a family legacy that filled our hearts with joy and purpose. "Let's start working on our community initiative this week," I suggested, excitement bubbling within me. "We can prepare a plan that aligns with your potential new role, making it a chance to showcase everything we've envisioned." Brody nodded, his enthusiasm matching mine. "I love that idea. We can brainstorm some outreach events that will highlight our combined strengths."

As the night drew on, I felt a peaceful certainty settle over me. The decision-making process regarding my career path, the potential challenges of Brody's job, and our commitments to Ethan felt like pieces in a larger puzzle coming together. With every passing moment, I understood that forging ahead meant embracing the unknown while remaining anchored in our love and partnership. The future was still unwritten, but I felt ready to embrace whatever came our way. Brody leaned in to kiss my forehead and wrapped his arms around me, I closed my eyes, breathing in the warmth of our shared space. This was where I belonged—right in the heart of our growing family, ready to forge forward into the brightness of tomorrow.

ANA MONROY

An Evening of Celebration

He stood in the kitchen, enveloped by the aroma of freshly sautéed garlic and herbs as he helped me to prepare dinner. The soft glow of candlelight flickered on the dining table, casting a warm and inviting ambiance, perfectly setting the stage for the significant evening ahead. Tonight was a special opportunity to celebrate his job offer, the recent triumphs, and the bond we had nurtured through our challenges. As he helped lay the table, I stirred the cooked pot which I had prepared, all a sudden a sense of satisfaction came over me.

Watching him flourish over the past few weeks had been incredible; his determination and ambition shone brighter than ever, filling me with pride for how far we had come together. Brody's presence when entering the kitchen area, made my face light up. "Wow, Ruby! That looks incredible," he exclaimed, his eyes sparkling with appreciation. His comments provided reassurance and affirmed me that celebrating our achievements was indeed the appropriate decision. "I wanted to celebrate our new opportunity and all the hard work we have accomplished," I replied, a smile spreading across my face. Moments like these reassured me of the strength of our relationship. "Oh, you didn't have to do all of this," he said, moving closer, sincerity lacing his voice. "But I want to," I insisted gently. "You deserve to be celebrated for everything you have achieved Brody. Tonight is about acknowledging not just your success but our journey together."

We settled in for dinner, the cozy atmosphere wrapped around us like a comforting embrace. I poured two glasses of red wine, savouring the intimate ambiance that enveloped us. As we shared bites of the delicious meal, laughter flowed effortlessly between us. He loved recounting cherished memories and discussing our hopes for the future.

Watching me talk animatedly about our aspirations filled him with pride. He wanted to help me harness our talent to its fullest potential. "I can't believe we're finally at this point," she said, my eyes aglow. "It truly feels like everything is falling into place." "I feel the same way," he replied, his heart swelling with gratitude. "You're on the cusp of something extraordinary, and I couldn't be prouder of you." "Thank you,

ANA MONROY

Brody," I said, my sincerity brightening the room. I reached across the table, intertwining my fingers with his, sending warmth, which radiated through his and reinforcing our bond. The connection between us deepened, and I could feel an exhilarating energy in the air, my excitement pushing him to dream even bigger about our future together.

Just as we began to solidify our plans, my phone buzzed against the table, breaking the flow of our warm conversation. Brody noticed my immediate change in demeanour, anticipation flickering in my eyes mixed with a hint of anxiety. "What is it?" He asked, his heart instinctively quickening. "It's a message from the hiring manager," he replied, his brow furrowing. "They want to meet with me tomorrow morning to discuss the outreach programme in more detail." My expression turned serious at his words. "Tomorrow morning? I replied. "They must be eager to finalize things, but I need to be prepared." "Off course," I said, trying to maintain my composure as I watched my excitement transform into anxiety.

We both worked so hard to carve out a space where our ambitions could thrive, and I did not want him to feel overwhelmed by the urgency. Just then, the doorbell rang again, jolting us from our cozy connection sitting at the kitchen table. "More interruptions tonight," he remarked lightly, even though he could sense the tension rising. "Do you want me to answer it, or would you prefer to see who it is?" I asked.

"I think it might be a guest coming to share in the celebration," he suggested, taking a deep breath to steady himself. "Alright, then," he said with a warm smile as he moved toward the door, I trailed closely behind, my heart still fluttering from the excitement of earlier. He swiftly opened the door; anticipation coursed through him. Standing outside the front door of his home was a representative from the office, someone who had come to discuss the recent developments regarding his role. "Brody!" he exclaimed, a bright smile lighting up his face. Brody turned back to me, noticing my shining smile in my eyes.

The evening was transforming from a celebratory dinner into a pivotal moment in all our lives, he felt gratitude for how this new opportunity was shaping our future. "Your hard work hasn't gone unnoticed," the representative continued, stepping inside. "The leadership team is thrilled this time with your potential, and they believe that your job promotion will play a crucial role in the direction of the company." He was awestruck, his face brightening with confidence from the encouraging news. Brody felt a sense of validation wash over him; all the late nights and relentless efforts had led to this very moment—an acknowledgment of our contributions and the promise of a bright new chapter. Ethan peeked around the corner, as he stood there, Ethan's curiosity piqued Brody's heart, and Brody knelt to face Ethan welcoming him to the conversation. "This is an important person from my work, Ethan. They are here to announce my promotion. "Really? That is impressive!" Ethan exclaimed, his face lighting up in awe. The pride in his voice filled me with warmth in my heart, reminding me of the important significance this promotion held for the entire family. "It's more than just a title," he explained, standing back up and looking at both me and Ethan. "This new role means I will have the opportunity to lead projects that can have influence in our community. It is a chance for us to all to grow together as a family while pursuing our passions."

As he saw the pride reflected in our faces, he knew this was more than just a career milestone; it was a step toward achieving our shared dreams. The representative continued, outlining the plans for Brody's new role and emphasizing how excited the leadership team was about integrating community engagement projects. Then suddenly my phone buzzed again, pulling my attention back to the present. Brody noticed an immediate change in my demeanour, and anxiety flickered across my face.

"What is it?" he asked, trying to gauge her reaction. "It's another message from the hiring manager," I said, my brow furrowing as I read the text. "They want to meet me tomorrow to discuss more about a possible vacant job role and they want me to apply for it." My excitement dimmed slightly, with worry creeping back in. "Tomorrow morning? He asked, they must really want to finalize things. But we need to be prepared for what they want to discuss." Brody replied.

"Absolutely," I nodded, my earlier enthusiasm now tinted with uncertainty. "After everything we've talked about tonight, it's important we go into this strategically." he intertwined his fingers with mine, grounding me in the moment. "Whatever happens next, we will navigate it together. Let us stay focused on our goals and our commitment to each other." An office representative suddenly left in a hurry. Brody kindly invited his friend from the outreach programme to sit with us at the kitchen table, he turned to his friend, leaning forward slightly. "What is going on? You seem urgent."

His friend's expression shifted by the weight of the important news. "I just got back from a meeting with some contacts who have been keeping an eye on you. They want to discuss all potential partnerships—projects that could align well with your talent and Ruby's recent successful outreach ideas." He exchanged glances at me, the spark of excitement igniting me again amidst the uncertainty. The possibilities seemed promising, yet Brody also felt the weight of the decisions at hand.

The evening marked a turning point, potentially redefining both our careers and family life. The night was still young, and as he turned back to his friend, he felt a renewed sense of hope. No matter what challenges lay ahead, he was ready to face them with me by his side, knowing that together we could navigate whatever came our way. I stepped back into the kitchen area, feeling a comforting warmth enveloping me as I re-entered the sanctuary I had come to cherish so deeply. After the whirlwind of emotions from the previous days, today truly felt like a celebrational moment to savour the love and connection that Brody and I had nurtured through challenges and triumphs.

Walking through the shared space, I admired the cozy atmosphere we had created together. The soft glow from the string lights strung delicately along the patio creating an inviting ambiance, twinkling like stars against the night sky. It was the perfect setting for the friendly gathering we were having—a blend of his friends and my own, all coming together to honour the new chapter in our lives. As I made my way back, I caught sight of Brody arranging snacks and drinks, his laughter blending effortlessly with the sounds of conversation drifting in from the backyard. The familiar faces of friends filled me with a sense of joy; it was comforting to see everyone gathering, their stories intertwining like the threads of a tapestry. "Hey, everything looks great!" I called out, stepping closer outside to help him. "Thanks! I wanted it to feel special," Brody replied, his warming gaze comforting my heart. "It's important to celebrate what we've built together, and I thought this gathering would be the perfect way to do it." This was not just a gathering; it was an affirmation of our relationship, an opportunity for our friends to witness the love we had cultivated. "I'm so glad we decided to do this."

As we all sat outside, the cool night air embraced us, and I took in the sight of his friends mingling, laughter ringing out under the soft glow of the lights in the backyard. The scene felt magical, illuminated by the gentle flicker of lanterns that danced in the night breeze. I spotted Ethan nearby, playing happily with his dino toy collection, his laughter echoing in the background.

The joy radiating from the friendly gathering warmed my spirit. It was a testament to the bond we had all formed—a community that would enrich our lives. Brody and I poured love to create a home that welcomed everyone who shared in our professional journey. The evening unfolded, I found myself immersed in conversations filled with hopes, dreams, and shared experiences. My heart felt full as I watched Brody connecting with his friends, his voice melancholy recounting stories that brought everyone closer. It was moments like these that reinforced our love we had for one another, reminding us of all we had overcome together. When it came time for a toast, I felt an electric thrill surge through my body.

Brody gathered all of us around, his eyes shining with enthusiasm. "To new beginnings, to the journeys we share, and to the love that brings us all together!" he proclaimed. With a cheer echoing around us, I raised my glass alongside Brody, the warmth of his connection enveloping me like a warm embrace. His laughter and chatter filled the space; I felt a deep sense of belonging. As the night wore on, I stole glances at Brody, who was animatedly engaging with his friend. I felt a profound sense of gratitude for this shared journey with Brody, for the love they we cultivated, and for the promise of what was yet to come. It was clear that life had a way of bringing people together, solidifying relationships, and crafting connections that could withstand the test of time. Toward the end of the evening, as the sky turned a deeper shade of navy and the stars twinkled above us, I took a moment to step back and take it all in. The camaraderie, the flickering lights—it painted a picture of happiness I wanted to hold onto forever. Taking Brody's hand, I felt grounded in that moment of celebration. "Thank you for everything," I whispered, sincerity pouring from my heart. "No, thank you for being you," Brody replied softly, squeezing my hand in return. "You've made this journey something spectacular."

In that beautiful moment, surrounded by friends, love, and the promise of a shared future, I felt an unwavering certainty. We had crafted a life together rich with connection, hope, and ambition, and I knew we were ready to embrace whatever awaited us. With a sense of joy and reassurance enveloping me, I realized that we had truly come home at last—not just to a place, but into each other's hearts.

With the twinkle of the stars above me and Brody's friend I felt prepared to embark on this path together with him, confident that our future would be filled with promises of better times together, with laughter, and love. As the evening continued, I felt the energy of the gathering wrap around me like the softest blanket. My heart swelled with gratitude as I watched him mingle with his friend, his charisma lighting up the space. There was something deeply satisfying about seeing his friends come together, united in celebration. When Ethan finished playing with his dino toys outside, he rushed over to me, holding a piece of chocolate cake that he had somehow snagged from the dessert table. "Auntie! Can we have another game after this? Everyone likes it!" he exclaimed, his eyes shining with enthusiasm.

"Of course, sweetie! After dessert," I replied, unable to suppress her smile. Moments like these filled her with warmth, anchoring her perspective on the balance between family, friendship, and ambition. I cherished the idea that they were building not just for us but also for Ethan's happiness, shaping his childhood with love and connection. As the outreach friend settled into casual conversations and the aroma of food wafted through the air, I caught a glimpse of Brody across the yard, animatedly discussing plans for the outreach programme initiative. Some pride surged within me he had such a way with people, effortlessly inspiring them with his vision.

I felt fortunate to have him by my side in all facets of life. I then turned to grab another drink; I heard laughter erupt behind me. When I glanced back, I realized it was Brody and his friend lifting their glasses for another toast, calling me to join in. Brody caught my eye and smiled, "Come on, Ruby!" he beckoned, his hands gesturing for mine to come closer. I made my way towards him, feeling as though I were moving into the heart of a celebration born from their collective efforts. As I stood beside Brody, he wrapped an arm around my shoulders, grounding me in the moment. "To friendship, love, and the journey we're all on together!" his friend announced, raising his glass high.

"Cheers!" I remarked while Brody lifting his own glass to join in. The sounds of clinking glassware mingled with laughter, and I felt a rush of pure joy. Here, surrounded by our favourite people, I recognized how vital these connections were. They were not just companions; they were integral parts of the tapestry of Brody's life, stitching together dreams and ambitions. As the night wore on, the music shifted to something softer, inviting gentle dancing to lighten the mood. He looked down at me, with a playful smile on his lips. "Shall we?" he asked, his heart fluttering in anticipation.

He grinned, taking my hand and leading me into the open space while swaying to the rhythm. With her heart beating in sync with the music, I felt as though we were stepping into our own little world, the warmth of the love wrapping around us. We danced; the outside world faded into the background. Brody pulled me closer, our bodies moving effortlessly as if they were two pieces of a larger puzzle. I gazed into his eyes, finding comfort. "Have I told you how proud I am of you?" Brody murmured, brushing a strand of hair behind my ear. "Not today," I teased, a gleam of mischief in my eyes. "Let me correct that," he said, his expression turning earnest. "I am incredibly proud of you for embracing this new opportunity and how you are ready to take it all on while keeping our family at the heart of it. You inspire me every day."

I felt warmth spread through me, grounding me in the moment as we swayed. "And you give me the confidence to pursue my dreams," I replied softly, her voice imbued with affection. Just then, my phone buzzed in my pocket once more, breaking the intimate spell that had enveloped us. I pulled it out, but when I saw the screen, my heart sank. It was a news alert about the job vacancy—something I did not want or need to process now.

"Everything alright?" Brody asked, noticing her change in demeanour. "It's just another update about the vacancy," I replied, feeling a sudden weight in my stomach. I hesitated, torn between the excitement of the evening and our shared moment. He reached for my hand, the warmth of his touch anchoring mine. "Focus on us right now. We'll deal with the outside world later," he reassured me, his emphasis on the "Us" reinforcing our bond. I looked into Brody's eyes and felt the shift within my determination to embrace the promises we had made to each other and to navigate whatever the future held together. As the music played on, and laughter echoed around us, my mind settled.

The evening continued to unfold in joyful harmony, the chatter echoing through the house long after the guest had departed. I felt a warm glow radiate from within me as I watched Brody and Ethan clean up together in the kitchen, their joyful banter filling the air. It was the kind of special moment that brought me immense satisfaction, manifestation of the love that suffused our home. As Ethan helped clear away the dishes, he suddenly turned to Brody, his face alight with excitement. "Dad, can we do this again next weekend? I want to show my friends how cool our home is and how my auntie is a superhero!" As the words left his mouth, my heart swelled with affection. I loved to witness the connection between the two and how proud Ethan was of his dad. "That sounds like a great idea, Ethan. I'd love to have another party," he replied, his voice full of warmth. Brody chuckled, ruffling Ethan's hair playfully. "I think we can make that happen, buddy. We'll brainstorm some fun ideas to include everyone." Once the kitchen was tidied, I leaned against the counter, my heart brimming with contentment. "Thank you for handling the cleanup," I said to Brody, my voice soft yet sincere. "It really means a lot to me." Brody turned to me; his eyes filled with affection. "You don't have to thank me for that, Ruby. We're a team, and I enjoy doing things together.

Plus, the celebration was your idea—I just wanted to help keep the momentum going." Thinking back to their earlier discussions with Brody, I felt a new sense of clarity and purpose surging within me. With the promise of my new opportunity ahead, I was more convinced than ever that we could strike the perfect balance between our ambitions and family life.

"Can I ask you something?" I ventured, taking a cautious step closer. "Of course," Brody replied, his gaze steady and encouraging. "Do you think we can genuinely make our dreams a reality, while also ensuring we're there for each other and for Ethan?" "Absolutely," he affirmed, reaching for her hand. "We'll lay the groundwork together. We can build something incredible while ensuring that our bond remains strong. I believe that's what will define our journey." Feeling inspired by his conviction, I squeezed his hand and smiled. "I can really see our future shaping up just like that. I'm so grateful for your support and insight".

As we settled down in the living room at nighttime, I felt an overwhelming sense of belonging, Brody's laughter filled our home with happiness and love. I watched him playfully engage with Ethan, their camaraderie a testament to the bond they had cultivated as a family. The worries that had once loomed overhead were fading fast, replaced by the warmth of our endeavours and promise of a brighter future. Later, as bedtime approached, I looked at Brody and Ethan nestled together on the couch, both laughing and enjoying the playful banter. In that moment, I felt a steadfast conviction in my heart. There was a sense of peace settling around me, I leaned in closer to Brody, whispering, "We really are building something special, aren't we?" Brody met my gaze, his eyes sparkling with love. "More than I ever dreamed possible," he replied softly.

I watched both feeling content that the journey ahead would only deepen our connection. This was our happy ever after home filled with laughter, love, and unbreakable bonds. With hearts intertwined and dreams unfurling before us, I felt an exhilarating rush of hope as we entered this new chapter of life together, confident that our commitment would lead us to a future overflowing with possibilities and joy, each day an affirmation of the love and life we had chosen together.

ANA MONROY

13

My Happy Ever After

I used to believe that happy endings only existed in fairy tales, the kind you read about when you're little, before life teaches you otherwise. But standing here now, watching Ethan giggle under the blanket fort we built in Brody's living room, I realized that maybe happiness ever afters look a little different in real life. Maybe they're quieter, less about sweeping gestures and more about the soft moments in between—the kind that sneak up on you when you're not looking. The sun dipped low through the windows, casting a warm golden light across the room. I leaned back against the couch cushion, blanket draped over my lap, watching Brody and Ethan wrestle over a plush dinosaur like it was a national treasure. There was joy here, in this room, that I hadn't felt in a long time. Not just happiness—but peace. A sense that I was exactly where I was meant to be. It didn't come easy. Brody's walls were high, and honestly, I had my own. I wasn't sure I could navigate the complexity of his life—an ex-partner, a demanding job, the ever-present tug-of-war between his responsibilities and his heart. But somewhere along the way, between staff meetings and pancake workshops, stolen glances and unexpected confessions, something shifted. We stopped pretending this connection wasn't real. And I fell—slowly, then all at once. I didn't fall just for Brody, though. I fell for Ethan. For his big curious eyes and his goofy dinosaur facts. For the way he called me "Aunt Ruby" before we were ever sure what we were. I fell for Sunday mornings in mismatched pyjamas, messy pancakes, and sleepy smiles. I fell for this little makeshift family we were piecing together. But the truth is, my happiness ever after wasn't just about them. It was about me, too.

Because for so long, I thought I had to prove something. That success had to look a certain way—spreadsheets, promotions, balance sheets in perfectly aligned cells. And while I'm proud of what I've built—of the workshop, the way the community embraced my ideas—none of it compares to the fulfilment I've found here. In being seen. In being loved. In building something meaningful with someone who never asked me to shrink or compromise to fit in his world.

"Ruby," Brody said, pulling me out of my thoughts. He crawled under the fort, hair tousled, cheeks flushed from laughing. "What are you thinking about over there?" I smiled. "Just… this. All of it." He raised an eyebrow. "That good, huh?" I laughed softly. "Better. I think I finally understand what home feels like." His expression shifted—softened in that way it only did when he let me see the real him. He reached out, taking my hand, his thumb brushing lightly over my knuckles. "You are home. For me. For Ethan. We didn't even know what we were missing until you came in." I blinked fast, willing the emotion in my chest to stay where it belonged. But it was too late—the tears welled, not from sadness, but from something deeper. Gratitude. Joy. Relief. I had spent so much of my life running toward something, chasing validation. And somehow, without even realizing it, I had run straight into everything I ever needed. Ethan popped his head out from behind a pillow. "Can we sleep in the fort tonight?" Brody and I exchanged a look and both answered in unison, "Of course." Later, as we all curled up under the fort—Ethan tucked between us, snoring softly—Brody leaned over and kissed my forehead. "Thank you," he whispered. "For what?" I whispered back. "For staying." I didn't answer right away. I just nestled closer, wrapping my arm around Ethan, my other hand resting against Brody's chest. I listened to the steady rhythm of his heartbeat beneath my fingertips. "I didn't stay," I finally said. "I chose this. I chose you."

That was my happiness ever after. The next morning started the way all my favourite ones did sunlight pouring through the sheer curtains, the smell of fresh coffee drifting in from the kitchen, and the soft sound of Ethan talking to his dinosaurs. I lingered in bed for a moment, just listening. I wasn't in a rush. I didn't need to be anywhere else. Brody peeked in, already dressed, holding a steaming mug. "You want cinnamon or vanilla today?" he asked with that crooked grin that never failed to make my chest flutter. "Surprise me," I said, stretching, my smile stretching with me. He walked in, sat beside me, and handed me the mug. "Ethan's setting the table. One fork, four spoons, and zero napkins so far. I think he's planning a cereal party." I laughed into my cup. "Sounds fancy. Should I change out of my pyjamas or is this a robe-and-slippers event?" "I think he'd approve of a crown, if you're willing."

It was in these small, ordinary mornings that I felt it most—that fullness I used to think only came with milestones or big announcements. But this was better. A sleepy child with a bowl too big for his hands. A man who kissed my shoulder before saying good morning. Laughter over coffee. Quiet joy. After breakfast, Ethan insisted we all go to the park— "Even if it's muddy," he declared, pulling on his mismatched socks with determined energy. So, we did. We chased him across the field, helped him build a lopsided stick fort near the trees, and listened to him explain the complex rules of a game he was clearly inventing as he went. Brody caught my hand in his while Ethan sprinted ahead, and we walked in sync down the gravel path. "You look happy," he said. "I am," I replied simply. "I didn't know I could be this kind of happy." He stopped walking, turned to face me. "Neither did I." There were still unanswered questions. Like what the future looked like. Whether we'd live here or start somewhere new. Whether I'd want children someday. Whether Jessica would always hover in the corners of our conversations. But none of those felt heavy anymore. They were just parts of the story we hadn't written yet.

That night, when Ethan had finally fallen asleep—his cheeks flushed from fresh air and chocolate chip cookies—Brody sat beside me on the couch, our feet tangled under a throw blanket. "I've been thinking," he said, a little nervously. "About what you said. About building something that lasts." I looked at him, curious. "I'm not rushing," he continued quickly, "but I've never been more certain of anything than I am about you. About us." "Me too," I said, and I meant it with every fibre of who I was now. "We don't have to figure it all out today," he said, reaching for my hand.

"But... I do know that I want you to wake up in this house. With me. With Ethan. If you'll have us." I leaned into him, resting my head against his chest, listening to the steady rhythm of his heart. "You already have me." And with that, something shifted—quiet and profound. Not a proposal. Not a promise wrapped in diamonds or fireworks. Just two people choosing each other, again and again, in all the small ways that mattered most. The life I had now didn't look like the one I'd once dreamed about. But it was real.

Deep. Messy. Beautiful. It was mine. And it was enough. But love has a way of unfolding in quiet layers, revealing more of itself the longer you live in it. That night, as Brody and I sat curled together on the couch, the hush of the house settling around us like a second skin, I realized just how much I had let go—of fear, of comparison, of the version of myself that thought love had to look a certain way to be real. "You're quiet," he said, brushing his thumb along the back of my hand. "I'm thinking," I murmured, smiling at the way my body naturally leaned into his. "About how much my life has changed." He nodded. "Mine too. For the better." I thought about the woman I used to be—always on the move, proving herself in boardrooms, chasing deadlines like they were lifelines. I'd built a fortress of competence around me, so thick I didn't even realize I was lonely inside it. And now, here I was, feet tangled with a six-year-old's socks in the laundry pile, my days anchored in peanut butter sandwiches and bedtime rituals. My heart had shifted without fanfare, but permanently.

The next few weeks flowed like a steady stream. No grand declarations. Just more of the same small, sacred things. Ethan started calling me "Roo," his own invented nickname that melted me every time. He'd say things like "Roo, can we have smiley pancakes today?" or "Roo, you're better at voices than Dad—can *you* read the dragon part?" I didn't correct him. I didn't question it. I just let it sink in.

One morning, while packing Ethan's lunch, Brody came up behind me and wrapped his arms around my waist. "You should bring some of your stuff over," he said casually, as if it weren't the most loaded suggestion in the world. I turned in his arms. "You mean... like a drawer? Or more?" He grinned. "More. All of it, if you want. I think Ethan already thinks you live here anyway. And, I mean, your toothbrush is already judging mine from the cup." I laughed. "It *is* a little judgmental." So, I did.

Over the course of a few weekends, my old apartment slowly emptied. Brody painted a wall in the guest room soft lavender— "just in case you ever want an office-slash-reading-nook-slash-hideout," he'd said with a wink. He cleared the space in the hallway closet. Ethan offered me three of his dinosaur figurines "for decoration," which I proudly arranged on the dresser beside my perfume. There was something so healing in the ordinariness of it all. One evening, we hosted dinner with friends from work. Lisa brought wine and Maggie brought a massive tray of homemade lasagna. We ate out on the deck under string lights, laughter echoing through the yard. Ethan wore his superhero cape the entire time and made everyone call him "Captain Pancake." At one point, while refilling drinks, I caught Brody looking at me from across the table. It wasn't a hungry, movie-scene gaze. It was gentler than that. Like he was quietly acknowledging the life we were living—and how far we'd both come to get here. After everyone left and the dishes were drying in the rack, Brody stood behind me at the sink, his hands slipping around my waist. "You fit," he said into my hair. "Not like you slid into a space that was already there—but like we built it around you." That night, I couldn't sleep. Not because I was anxious, but because my mind wouldn't stop cataloguing the hundred small things that had brought me to this moment.

I thought about my mother, about how she used to say, "Don't rush the middle, baby. That's where the real life is." And I understood now what she meant. Because this was the middle. And it was magic. A few days later, as we walked through the local farmer's market—Ethan holding my left hand and a giant apple cider donut in the other—Brody turned to me out of the blue. "You know, Ethan starts school full-time this fall." "I know," I said, stealing a bite of his donut while Ethan was distracted by a golden retriever in a costume.

"We'll have more time. Just us." I nodded, curious. "I was thinking maybe we could travel. Just a little. Take that trip you've always wanted to do. Portugal, wasn't it?" I blinked. "You remembered." "Of course I remembered." He squeezed my hand. "You're my home now, but I want to see the world with you too. I want Ethan to see it with us." That night, I tucked Ethan into bed. He curled into me sleepily. "Roo, are you going to live with us forever now?" I hesitated, not because I didn't know the answer, but because I felt the weight of his tiny question. "Yeah, baby," I whispered. "Forever sounds pretty perfect to me." He smiled without opening his eyes. "Good. I like it when we're all together." Me too. As I slipped into bed beside Brody, the air cool and the covers warm, I realized I'd found something I never thought I'd have—*not just love*, but a *life* built from it. A real, sturdy, imperfect, joyful life. I reached for his hand beneath the blankets. "I've been thinking," I said, echoing the way he always started his most meaningful sentences. "Oh?" he teased, turning to face me. "I want to build more. Not just this house, or this family. I want all of it. The hard parts. The boring days. The new adventures." "You sure?" I nodded. "I'm all in." His smile was slow and certain. "Then let's do it. One messy, beautiful day at a time." Later, as the evening settled into quiet, I watched Brody from across the room. He was staring out the window, his brow furrowed just a little as he lost himself in thought. "Hey," I called softly. He turned, a gentle smile curving his lips. "Yeah?"

"Do you ever think about the future?" "Every day," he said. "I think about how I'm not so scared of it anymore." "You used to be, huh?" "Yeah. I guess I thought that living through the past meant I'd miss the present. But I'm seeing now that maybe... maybe the best part of the future is learning to just live in the now. With you. With Ethan." I walked over to him, wrapping my arms around his waist, pressing myself to the warmth of him. "You don't have to do it all by yourself anymore." "I know. That's what you've taught me." We stood there together for a long time, breathing in sync, taking in the quiet certainty of the moment. And in that stillness, I realized something else, this was my happiness ever after.

Not because everything was perfect, but because I didn't need perfect anymore. I just needed this. The next morning, after a breakfast of pancakes, bacon, and more coffee than any of us should drink, I watched as Brody helped Ethan get his shoes on. My heart swelled with something I couldn't quite name. When we stood in the doorway, ready to take on the day, Brody turned to me one last time, a grin tugging at his lips. "So, Portugal, huh?" I laughed. "Maybe sooner than you think." And at that moment, I knew—I was exactly where I needed to be. Not just with him, but with us. And I was never, ever leaving.
The weeks that followed were filled with a quiet, unspoken joy that I didn't know was possible. We fell into a rhythm, one that felt natural but still magical. It wasn't always easy—life still had its bumps—but the way Brody and I leaned into each other, and the way Ethan's laughter echoed through the house, made everything feel a little lighter. We planned our trip to Portugal, piece by piece, savouring the anticipation of a shared adventure. Brody took on the role of excited planner, making lists and researching little villages, while I revelled in the idea of seeing the world through the eyes of a child, showing Ethan places where history and beauty lived in the quiet corners. We mapped out the days, knowing that the true gift was simply being together.

One evening, as I sat with Brody on the couch, a glass of wine in my hand and the soft hum of the world outside our window, he turned to me with that look again—the one that made everything inside me flutter. "You know," he said, voice steady, "I was thinking... the best part of this life, this family, this love—it's that we just keep adding to it. It's not about getting everything perfect or making sure we have all the answers. It's just about showing up for each other. Every day." I leaned into him, the warmth of his body a comfort I never wanted to let go of. "I think I've known that for a while now. And I think the best part is that we've already built the best part of our future, just by being here." His hand found mine, fingers twining together naturally. "You know, I used to think a family was just a small, tight-knit thing. But now, with you and Ethan... it's bigger than that. It feels like the whole world is ours to explore." I smiled at my heart full. "The world, huh?" He chuckled, his lips grazing my temple. "Yeah. Why not? We've got the best team." And with that, we moved forward together, one day after another. Each moment, no matter how simple, was steeped in love.

There were weekends at the park with laughter and picnic sandwiches. Late-night conversations where we talked about dreams and fears and the quiet, unspoken promise that we'd face it all together. Ethan's school year came to an end, and we celebrated with ice cream cones and handmade cards. He was growing—too fast for my liking—but every milestone was a new chance to hold onto this life. The summer we'd planned our Portugal trip arrived. We boarded the plane together, the excitement palpable. Ethan couldn't stop talking about the "mystery animals" he hoped to find in the streets of Lisbon, and Brody kept pointing out every little detail he thought might interest me—the narrow alleyways, the pastel-coloured buildings, the promise of warm beaches. And, in those moments, I realized something. This was my version of happy ever after. Not a distant, unreachable fantasy. Not an image of perfection. But something I could touch, feel, live in every day. The small moments, the laughter-filled mornings, the quiet evenings spent talking about everything and nothing at all, the comfort of knowing we didn't have to try so hard anymore because we had each other.

We made it. All of us. In our own messy, imperfect way. And that, I realized as we walked together through the cobbled streets of Lisbon, was exactly what I needed. The world was wide and full of possibilities, but wherever we went, if we were together, I knew we were already home. So, here it was. My happy ever after. Not because everything was perfect. But because it was real. And because I had found exactly where I belonged. With them. All in. Every single day.

ANA MONROY

14

A New Beginning

Years passed, and the city around us continued to hum with its relentless energy, but for us, time seemed to slow down, wrapping us in a cocoon of love and stability we never thought we'd find. The space that once felt so uncertain had transformed into a home—one that was filled with laughter, tenderness, and the quiet understanding that we were enough, just as we were. Brody and I found our rhythm in ways I never could've imagined. The early days of uncertainty, when I'd worried about fitting into a life that wasn't mine, seemed like a distant memory now.

We had built something so much stronger than I'd ever thought possible. Our love, as messy as it had been, had turned into something solid, something that could withstand anything. Ethan was growing fast, too fast for my liking, but I had learned to embrace every phase of his life. From the little boy who needed me for everything to the teenager who still needed me, just in quieter, subtler ways, I had been there every step of the way. His laughter still filled the house, but now, it was often accompanied by deep thoughts about the world, dreams for his future, and a sense of independence I knew he would need one day. Brody, as always, was my constant. His smile had become my anchor, his quiet strength my foundation. Together, we navigated the complexities of co-parenting Jessica, the ebbs and flows of our work lives, and the little bumps in the road that life had thrown our way. But no matter what, we had always come back to each other, every time.

ANA MONROY

We had long ago left behind the idea that love had to be perfect. We had accepted that imperfection was part of it, that even the messiest of moments had a place in our story. I had learned to love all of it—the moments of joy, the moments of frustration, the compromises, and the surprises. There was no such thing as "the perfect love," but there was something so much more beautiful: a real, tangible connection. A life built together, piece by piece. We had also created a home for Jessica, though it wasn't always easy.

At times, there were tensions when I questioned whether we were doing enough to make her feel secure, times when I struggled with the complicated feelings of co-parenting with someone who once part of Brody's past was. But in the end, we had made it work. We had all found a way to build a shared family, one that was messy and imperfect, but real. In the years that followed, we took that trip to Portugal—just like we had planned. It was everything we hoped for and more. Ethan was fascinated by the old-world charm of the streets, the history that seemed to be woven into the very stones, and the new flavours he eagerly embraced. Brody and I shared quiet moments, tucked into cafes, sipping espresso and savouring the simple joy of being together. We returned home with a collection of memories—photographs, postcards, stories—but also something more intangible: a deeper bond, an unspoken understanding of just how far we'd come.

At home, the days turned into months, and months into years. Brody and I continued to build our lives together, balancing everyday with the extraordinary. There were anniversaries, birthdays, and quiet nights at home. There were also difficult conversations, but they were always followed by resolutions. We had learned that the key to love wasn't in avoiding the hard things, but in facing them together. I had stopped looking for fireworks and grand declarations, because I had learned the greatest truth of all: love wasn't about the big, sweeping moments. It was about the small, quiet ones, the way Brody's hand brushed against mine when we were cooking dinner, the way Ethan asked me to help him with his homework even though he was old enough to do it on his own. It was about those little gestures that spoke louder than words ever could.

We had built our own definition of "happily ever after." It wasn't without challenges, but it was ours, and that was enough. As I stood in the kitchen one evening, stirring a pot of soup while Brody set the table and Ethan worked on his guitar in the living room, I realized how far we'd come. I wasn't the same woman who had walked into this life years ago, uncertain of what I was looking for. I was someone who had found love—not in the way I'd expected, but in the way that mattered most.

ANA MONROY

Through the quiet moments, through the ups and downs, through the building of something strong and steady, I had found exactly what I needed: a place where I belonged.

We didn't need fireworks to define our love anymore. We had built a life full of moments, of laughter, and of a love that was more real than anything I could have ever dreamed of. And as I looked around, at the people who had become my world, I knew I had found my happy ever after. Not because it was perfect—but because it was ours. The end was never the end. It was just the beginning of something even more beautiful. The quiet hum of the city seemed to echo in the background as me and Brody sat on their porch, sipping their coffee as the sun rose over the horizon. It was a typical Saturday morning, but there was a weight in the air that neither of them could shake. I noticed it first. "Brody?" she began, her voice soft but laced with curiosity, "What's been on your mind lately?" He set his mug down, his fingers tracing the rim absentmindedly. "Just... everything. Work's been overwhelming, and I've been thinking about what comes next. For us, for Ethan... I just don't want to mess this up. I don't want to take things for granted."

My heart ached at the vulnerability in his voice. It wasn't often Brody let himself feel vulnerable in front of her. He had always been the rock, the one who kept everything together. "I don't think you're messing anything up," I said, my hand reaching out to gently squeeze his. "You're here. You're present. That's more than enough." He smiled weakly, but she could tell there was something deeper troubling him. It was more than just the pressures of work. It was the unspoken fear of the future—the fear that they might not be able to keep everything balanced, that life might throw something their way they couldn't handle.

"We've been doing well, haven't we?" I continued, my eyes searching for his. "We've built something beautiful, and I'm not going anywhere. We've got this." Brody nodded, but his gaze was distant, as if his mind was elsewhere. "I know, Ruby. I know. But sometimes I wonder if... if I'm doing enough for Ethan. He's growing so fast, and I can't help but feel like I'm not enough. That I'm not enough for him, or for you." I took a deep breath, my mind racing. This wasn't just about Ethan. This was about Brody's fear of inadequacy, his fear of not being enough, not only for his son, but for her too. "You're enough, Brody. You've been more than enough from the start," I said, her voice steady but full of warmth. "We're a team, remember? And we always have been." Brody looked at her then, his expression softening, and for a moment, I could see the storm of emotions behind his eyes. It was a look I knew well. I had seen it before—when he'd lost his wife through divorce, when he'd been at his lowest. But this time, there was something different. There was hope. "I don't want to just survive this life, Ruby," he said, his voice tight with emotion. "I want to thrive. I want to give Ethan everything I didn't have when I was growing up. And I want to give you everything you deserve. You and I... we've both been through so much, but I want to build something that's permanent. Something real." My heart swelled at his words. I could feel the sincerity in every syllable, and it struck her deeply. It wasn't just about providing for their family—it was about creating a future, one that was rooted in love and trust.

"I want that too," I said, my voice unwavering. "We've already started something beautiful, Brody. We've created a home for Ethan, and we've built a foundation for us. But what do we do now? What's next?" Brody leaned back in his chair, his hand still resting on hers, and for a moment, they both stared out at the city skyline. There was a certain weight to his question, a quiet seriousness that hung in the air. They both knew the answer, it was time to take a leap, to move beyond just surviving and into living. "I think it's time we figure out what we really want. What we're building together," Brody said, his voice filled with conviction. "We've spent so much time focusing on the present, and now it's time to look ahead. I want to take the next step with you, Ruby. But we need to be sure about what that step is."

I smiled softly, feeling my heart race with anticipation. This was it. This was the conversation that would shape the future of their relationship. This was the moment that would define our next chapter. "Then let's dream together," I said, my words slow and deliberate, as if I was savouring each one. "Let's talk about what we want—not just for us, but for Ethan too. What kind of future do we want to give him?" Brody's eyes softened as he looked at me, a spark of excitement lighting up his gaze. "What if we bought a house? A place of our own. Somewhere we could build a future for Ethan, for us... a place we can call home. Not just a house, but a home. A family home. I felt the weight of his words settle over me like a soft blanket. I had always dreamed of having a place to call my own, a space where I could create lasting memories with the people I loved most. And now, the idea of building that life with Brody—of creating something tangible, something lasting—seemed like the perfect next step. "That sounds like exactly what we need," she said, her voice filled with warmth. "But what about... us? What do we want for our relationship? I don't want to lose sight of that, either." Brody looked at me, his expression softening with understanding. "I want to keep growing with you. I don't want to stop learning from each other. We've been through a lot, but I believe in us, Ruby. I believe we can face whatever comes next." I smiled, a tear slipping down my cheek. I wiped it away quickly, not wanting him to see the emotion that swelled in my heart. "I believe in us too." And in that moment, we both knew that whatever came next, we would face it together. Our bond was unbreakable. Our love, steady and sure. We had built something real, and together, we would continue to build on that foundation, step by step, dream by dream. As we sat there, the sun rising higher in the sky, we knew that the journey wasn't over. That it was just the beginning.

15

Epilogue Part One: A Home of Our Own

ANA MONROY

I never thought a front porch could feel sacred, but here I am—barefoot, cup of chamomile tea in hand, the fading sun brushing gold across the sky—and I can't imagine being anywhere else. Brody's laugh echoes from inside the house. It's low and familiar and it settles into my chest like it belongs there. Through the screen door, I catch a glimpse of him chasing Ethan down the hallway with a dish towel, both howling with laughter, their voices a duet of chaos and joy. This is our life now. A beautiful, unpolished mosaic of pancake mornings, lost socks, impromptu dance parties, and bedtime rituals that always include "just one more" story. It's not pristine. It's not curated. But it's mine. Ours. And it's perfect in all ways that matter. I step back inside and set my mug on the counter. There are crumbs from this morning's cinnamon toast, a crayon drawing of our house stuck to the fridge, and Ethan's latest school project—a popsicle stick robot—leaning at a dangerous angle by the sink. I used to flinch at disorder. Now I smile. The mess tells me we're alive. The clutter tells me we're here. Brody corners me by the kitchen island, his arms wrapping around my waist from behind. He smells like soap and pizza dough, and I never get tired of how easily I fold into him. "What are you smiling at?" he murmurs, kissing my temple. "You," I say. "Us. This." He rests his chin on my shoulder. "I keep thinking one day I'll wake up and this will all be a dream." "Nope." I reached up and touched the side of his face. "This is real. This is ours." Later, after Ethan's tucked in—curled around his stuffed triceratops, dreaming out loud about flying space dinosaurs—we settle onto the back porch wrapped in a blanket, the night air crisp but comforting.

Brody takes my hand, and there's something different in his grip tonight. Not nervousness. Something steady. Certain. "I've been thinking about the future," he says. "Oh?" I arch a brow, teasing. "You're not usually the planner between us." He grins. "Touché. But I was thinking… what if we started looking for a place of our own? A bigger space. Maybe with a yard for Ethan to run wild in. You can make a mess in the kitchen. An office for your business. A room we could turn into a nursery one day…" His words trail off, giving me space to react. But I don't hesitate. My heart knows the answer before my mind catches up. "Yes," I whisper. "To all of it." His shoulders relax, the quiet exhale of a man who's been holding a hope close to his chest. "And maybe next year," he adds softly, "we could make it official. You and me. Rings, vows. The works." Tears prick at my eyes, not from surprise, but from relief. From joy. I pressed my forehead on his. "I thought you'd never ask. "I was waiting until the moment felt right." "It does," I say, voice thick with emotion. "It really,

really does." We sit in silence then, listening to the distant chirp of crickets and the wind brushing through the trees. The stars blink overhead, and I swear the sky itself is smiling

16

Epilogue Part Two: Three Years Later

The house is louder these days. Between Ethan's eight-year-old giggles echoing through the hallways, a barking rescue puppy named White Socks thinks he runs the place, there is a distant hum of Brody singing off-key in the shower while making up rhymes about scrambled eggs—this is not the quiet life I once thought I wanted. It's so much better. Three years ago, I stood barefoot in Brody's kitchen, pouring pancake batter shaped like hearts and dinosaurs, thinking maybe—just maybe—this was the beginning of something lasting.

I had no idea what would come next. I didn't know that "lasting" would mean shared bills and grocery lists, first grade science projects, fights over who forgot to take the recycling out, and long, quiet nights wrapped in each other's arms while the baby monitor crackled nearby. Yes. Baby monitor. Because somewhere between the early Saturday morning soccer practices and late-night giggle fits, Brody and I decided to grow our family. Not out of pressure. Not because it was expected. But because the love in this home had outgrown its corners. We had room—space in our lives, our hearts—for one more. Our daughter, Isla, came into the world on a warm June morning, and nothing has been the same since. She has Brody's dimples and my tendency to frown when she's thinking hard. She's pure magic, and Ethan? He's the best big brother I could have imagined. Overprotective, patient (mostly), and convinced he's already teaching her to walk, even though she's barely sitting up.

Brody proposed to me on a rainy Wednesday in our living room. There were no fancy candles or sweeping gestures. Just us, in our pyjamas, folding laundry, with Ethan shouting from the kitchen, "Are you going to say yes or what?" I laughed so hard I cried. And then I said yes—of course I said yes. The wedding was small. Backyard. String lights. Close friends. Ethan stood proudly beside Brody as our "Best Little Man," and when Brody read his vows, there wasn't a dry eye in sight. He didn't promise perfection. He promised presence. Honesty. Patience. Late-night cups of tea. Pancake Saturdays. A life built, not bought.

A family chosen and cherished. Sometimes I still wake up expecting the other shoe to drop. But when I open my eyes and see Brody—hair wild, breath slow, arm flung over a pillow—and hear Isla gurgling through the baby monitor, or the muffled sound of Ethan brushing his teeth with the bathroom door wide open, I know this isn't a dream. This is our life. Messy. Warm. Wonderfully, beautifully real. We didn't get here easily. We stumbled through miscommunications, old wounds, co-parenting complications, and fears that love this good couldn't last. But we did the work. Together. And now, here we are. Three years later, on a Sunday morning, sipping lukewarm coffee in a sweatshirt that used to be Brody's, watching Ethan teach Isla how to stack her soft blocks into a leaning tower while Niblet snores beside them, I feel it all over again. Gratitude. Peace. Joy. Love, the slow kind. The staying kind. My happy ever after. And it's everything I never knew I always wanted.

ANA MONROY

https://www.amazon.co.uk/review/create-review?&asin=B0F4XYW7X7

ANA MONROY

Acknowledgments

This book is dedicated to my father John Monroy and late mother Jane Sylvester who have been my inspiration throughout my life on and off, they have always believed in me to always follow my dreams.

ANA MONROY

ANA MONROY

Authors Note

A Tapestry of Promises is a millionaire, age gap, childhood sweetheart, forced proximity, boss romance novel. It is written for the Contemporary Romance reader in mind full of sweet moments and insight into the lives of these characters with some scenes that may be for only adult readers. I hope you will love to like my book about Ruby White and Brody Carter's relationship as much as I do. This is my first among perhaps a series of books later to be published in the coming year. A Tapestry of Promises contains mature content that may not be suitable for all audiences.

ANA MONROY

Ana Monroy

Born in London, Ana Monroy discovered a passion for storytelling later in life, embarking on her literary journey in her early forties. After enrolling in a short creative writing course taught by Karla Marie, she found both encouragement and inspiration to pursue fiction writing with heart and purpose. Specializing in contemporary romance with strong, complex women at the forefront, her debut novel explores themes of love, healing, and finding home in unexpected places. Blending emotional depth with everyday magic, her stories resonate with readers who believe that it's never too late to rewrite your own narrative. She hopes to continue crafting heartfelt, character-driven novels that speak to women at all stages of life. This book is available in both e-Kindle format and paperback. For updates on upcoming releases, signings, or just to connect, you can follow her online.

ANA MONROY

"When one is in love, one always begins by deceiving oneself, and one always ends by deceiving others. That is what the world calls a romance,"

ANA MONROY

"I think the best thing you can do is just love someone and take a chance,"

Agatha Christie

ANA MONROY

ANA MONROY

ANA MONROY

ANA MONROY

Printed in Dunstable, United Kingdom